Harmony & Choas
A Jersey Love Affair

A Note From The Author

I decided not to do a dedication and acknowledgment this time around. Reason being is because so many people that I acknowledged in the past turned out to be toxic. I don't want to make the mistake in acknowledging those who aren't deserving of it. I also don't want to give oxygen to dead situations. Just know if you're my true few and you support me then I love you, simple.

-IAmRedsJohnson
#ISlayBooks

Prologue

"What the fuck!" Chaos stormed up the stairs, hopping up two steps at a time into the master bedroom, and looked at Harmony as she laughed hysterically.

Harmony had just thrown a fifth of Henny on him and he was beyond pissed. She took it as a joke because she knew just how to get under his skin and bring him out of character.

"Don't what the fuck me. Who was that bitch texting your phone?" she asked through pursed lips, with her arms folded across her chest.

"Wasn't no bitch texting my phone. The fuck you coming at my neck for anyway? You got niggas coming at you on a daily!"

Harmony waved him off. It was just like Chaos to flip the script on her but, over the years of dealing

with him, Harmony had gotten used to it, so it wasn't as easy for him to get to her as it was before.

"I don't wanna hear that shit. You either gon' tell me who the fuck that bitch is, or I will GPS her number and I'll find out who the fuck she is myself," Harmony warned.

Chaos wiped his hand down his face as he looked at his woman. He knew she was good to pull up on a bitch if need be. He didn't want anyone to get their ass beat over an innocent text message, so he just confessed.

"Baby, it wasn't like that. She's just an old friend who decided to hit me up and see how I was doing. You need to stop fucking tripping. You know you my one and fucking only. Ya guts is the only one's I'm beating down, believe that," Chaos said as he pulled his wife beater over his head and threw it on the floor.

She watched as he unbuckled his jeans and dropped them to his knees, along with his brief boxers. His thick nine-and-a-half-inch anaconda stood at attention. She just knew he was about to punish her pussy by the way it was staring at her.

"The fuck you over there drooling for? You ain't getting none of this good dick after what you done did. I'm about to hop in the tank. As a matter of fact, sit down on the bed and think about what you've done." Chaos headed towards the bathroom doorway before he heard Harmony suck her teeth.

He laughed and went into the bathroom, shutting the door behind him. He knew she was pissed because she couldn't get any dick, but she was just going to have to be mad because he had things to do at the club later. Chaos let the water run over his body for a few before lathering up his wash cloth with some of his AXE body wash. He cleaned himself from head to toe and then rinsed his body. He turned the water off and stepped out of the shower, wrapping a towel around his waist. Chaos wiped the fog off the mirror and admired himself. His fresh line-up he had gotten earlier had him looking like new money. But, that was nothing new because even on his worse day, he looked like a million bucks. Chaos grabbed his toothbrush and toothpaste and quickly brushed his teeth. When he was done, he swished some mouth wash around in his mouth and then spit it out.

"Ahhhh," he made a noise as he stuck out his tongue.

Chaos walked back into the bedroom to find Harmony watching tv.

"Where you going?"

"To the club. Don't ask me a question you already know the answer to."

Harmony rolled her eyes. She watched Chaos drop his towel and expose that pretty chocolate dick of his. The veins were bulging as it stood out at attention. He rubbed Cocoa Butter on his body and then threw on a clean pair of boxer briefs.

"You need to control your dick. That's why those bitches always on you because your dick always hard."

Chaos chuckled. "Kind of explains the way I got you."

Harmony threw the remote control to the side and hopped off the bed. A few steps later, she was standing in back of Chaos, blowing nothing but hot air as she fussed at him.

"Don't say no stupid shit like that nigga! I def' wasn't on your dick like these thirsty, popcorn ass

bitches be. I'm above all. Don't even compare me to them whack ass bitches!"

Chaos smiled inside because he was pushing her buttons and he knew it. *Bet she won't throw shit else on me*, he thought.

"Ssss, ouch!" he winced in pain when Harmony pinched him in his side. It was like she could hear his thoughts. The pinch was followed by a punch in his back.

"Stop fucking hitting me. Then, when I knock your fucking head, off I'll be wrong." He slipped into a pair of red, knee-length basketball shorts with black lining and a black, v-neck t-shirt.

"I wish you would hit me! I wish you would nigga!" she taunted.

Chaos ignored her and put on his white and black Nike socks, along with his black Adidas slippers.

"Why the fuck you got on Nike socks with Adidas?"

Chaos glanced at her. "Because I'm that nigga and I can do that. Anymore fucking questions?"

He wasn't big on following the rules. He always stepped outside of the box and did what other niggas

was afraid to do. Clearly, he was the type that would wear two different brand clothing and not give the slightest fuck about it.

"I guess so but, anyway, what time you gon' be back?" Harmony looked at her cellphone and saw that it was already going on 8:30 p.m.

She couldn't stand when Chaos went to the club, let alone at night time because that's when all the wanna-be thugs would come there and try to act up. Most of all, that's when the bitches got extremely out of pocket because the majority of the ballers came in at night.

"I'm not sure at the moment. You know tonight is Kevin Gates' party, so I gotta get there now to finish puttin' shit together."

"So, why you got on lounging clothes?" she asked.

"Brave already got my outfit at the club. I wanted to go to the club in something comfortable because I gotta finish puttin' shit together, like I just said."

Harmony sighed because she wanted him to stay in with her tonight, but this was one of the biggest parties he'd had, so she had to let him handle his business.

Chaos put on some of his Versace cologne and then turned around to face his lady. He walked up on her and grabbed the sides of her face with his hands in an aggressive but romantic manner.

"You know I love your wild ass, right?" He shared his tongue with her.

Harmony took it with no problem. She loved the taste of him, but her wants caused her to betray him time and time again. "Yeah, I know, but you better get going. The sooner you leave, the quicker you will return."

Chaos gave her another peck on the lips. "Yeah, I hear you." He walked out of the bedroom and she followed behind him. "Give me a chance to peep things and I'll hit you up in a little while."

Harmony handed him his keys to his 2015 all-white Bentley and kissed him once more. "Alright, make sure you do. I love you."

"Love you more." Chaos left out of the house.

Harmony looked out of their bay window and watched as he got in his car and pulled off. She bit her bottom lips, watching his car until the tail light was out of sight. She planned on telling Chaos the

truth that night, but she couldn't muster up the strength to do it.

I'll just do it when he gets back, she thought.

She plopped down on the couch and cuddled up in fetal position, reaching for the remote on the end table and powering on the tv. She settled to watch VH1's hit movie, The Breaks, before dropping the remote by the couch on the floor. Harmony laid down and drifted off to sleep, not realizing she was tired.

An hour later, she was awakened by the ringing of the house phone.

Ring. Ring. Ring

Harmony hadn't even realized she had fallen asleep. She sat up on the couch and wiped the drool from her cheek. She instantly became aggravated because of the loud ringing. It was rare that their house phone rung but, when it did, the noise bothered her.

"Hello!" she yelled into the phone. Her voice cracked from the left over sleep.

"Yo, Harmony, Chaos got shot! I mean, that nigga got shot bad. He bleeding bad. Man, all this shit is bad!" Brave said in a panicked tone.

Harmony's heart dropped into her stomach. She couldn't believe the news she'd just received. At that moment, the room started to spin, her head got dizzy, and her vision became cloudy. Her mouth watered and she swallowed hard to keep the vomit that was forcing its way up, down.

She knew there was a reason she didn't want him to go to the club that night. Her gut told her that something would happened, but she didn't listen. Harmony didn't know that, when she told Chaos she loved him, it would be her last time able to do it.

REDS JOHNSON

Chapter One

Harmony Chardonnay Winfield-Miller, a beautiful sistah. Her beauty was mesmerizing. Five foot six and a petite little thing, but she held the right amount of weight in the right places. Beautiful eyes, full lips, and her silky, smooth, chocolate coco skin was radiate. Harmony was a breath of fresh air and she could have any man she wanted. She was a hard working woman, but she couldn't front and act like she didn't use what she had to get what she wanted.

She pulled up to her business building in her all-white 2014 Chevy Impala. Harmony was twenty-seven years old and she owned her own business, which was *Love and Harmony Boutique.* She thought the name would be a perfect fit to express her love for fashion and nice things. When Harmony got out of her car, she could see through the glass windows that business was running smooth today. It was a Thursday afternoon and customers were already pouring in and out. She loved to see the ladies wear her latest styles in fashion. Everything was well thought out from the minds of her and approved by her love, the one and only Chaos.

"Good afternoon Mrs. Winfield," one of her workers named Crystal greeted her.

"Good afternoon honey. It looks like today is going well so far."

Crystal gave her a warm smile in response to what she said. Harmony greeted a few of her customers before heading to the back to her office. She placed her purple Tory Burch bag on her love seat, before sitting down at her desk. She immediately checked her messages and missed calls. After responding back to the ones that were important, Harmony fished through the paperwork that was stacked on her desk. She had a few meetings with some important designers that she was indecisive on doing. She enjoyed doing her own thing and having her own brand, and she didn't want to gain clout off anyone else.

Ring. Ring. Ring

Harmony heard the ringing of her phone and slid her swivel chair back. She got up and went to her bag and pulled out her cellphone. Her heart melted when she saw Chaos' picture flash across the screen, along with his name.

"Hello handsome," she purred.

"What it do beautiful?" His deep voice made her heart do a special melody for him.

Harmony sat back down at her desk. "Nothing much. I'm just sitting here going through some paperwork. I have to order a few more things for the store, clothing included."

"You got that or you need my help?"

Harmony smiled. "Ordering wise or money wise?"

"Whatever you need ma, I got you."

Chaos was everything and then some to Harmony. They had been together for six years and there wasn't a day that went by that she didn't love him more and more. He was hardcore, but he had a soft spot when it came to her. She loved him dearly and there wasn't anything she wouldn't do for him.

"Why you being so nice today?" she joked, as if this wasn't him on a daily.

"Stop it ma. You already know how a nigga do when it comes to you."

"Yeah, yeah, I know. I was just messing with you. But, who is that in the background? Don't make me have to cut a bitch."

It was nothing for Harmony to go from 0 to 100 real quick. When it came to her man, any bitch could get it, including his mother. She had put in too much time and work with him to let another bitch slide up and try to take what was hers.

"Yo, chill with all that. I'm at the club and you know it's a lot of bitches here. I shouldn't have to keep explaining that none of these bitches mean a damn thing to me. Why the fuck would I want a bitch that shake her ass for a million niggas, when I can come home to you every night and have you all to myself?"

Harmony calmed down and blushed. "I know that. But, she just sounded a bit too close for my taste. Anyway, what do you want for dinner tonight?"

She listened as Chaos was speaking to a male in the background. Feeling a bit disrespected that he didn't even tell her to hold on, she sucked her teeth.

"My fault. But, um, I'll probably grab something while I'm out or, if you do cook something, just put my plate up because I won't be coming home tonight."

Harmony rolled her eyes, as if Chaos could see her do it through the phone. "Really Chaos? I understand that you're the owner of the club, but do you really have to be there all night?"

"You also know that it's Thursday. Thursday, Friday, and Saturdays are busy as fuck for the club, so don't try me. Not today and, matter of fact, not any other day. You know I'm the head nigga in charge around here and shit don't move until I say move it."

"Fine. Just give me a call later then. I love you," she said, not wanting to go back and forth any further.

"Love you more."

Click.

Chaos ended the call and Harmony threw her phone on her desk and covered her face with her hands. She sighed as she shook her head. Harmony loved Chaos, but work seemed to come between their relationship at times. They were both bosses of their businesses, but Chaos always took things to another level when it came to work. He always spent unnecessary time at the club, when he had a right hand man who was also his partner and a handful of workers he trusted enough to make sure things ran smoothly.

Knock. Knock. Knock

Harmony looked up to see Jasmin, another one of her workers, walk through her door.

"Hey, Mrs. Winfield. I'm just getting back from lunch. I see that Crystal and Renee have things under control. Did Crystal let you know that we need a few more things in stock? The Maxi dresses are sold completely out."

Harmony was pleased to see how Jasmin and Crystal were on top of things, but what she didn't like was how Renee had been acting lately.

"I'm aware of everything, thank you. But, can you please send Renee to my officer please," she said politely.

"Sure, no problem. Let me know when you make the orders and when the arrival date is. Oh, what the hell. I know you will let me know." Jasmin laughed as she left Harmony's office.

Harmony chuckled at how ditzy Jasmin was. She began to go through some more paperwork. She didn't get but a few pages in sorting out different orders that needed to be made before Renee stormed into her office.

"You wanted something?" she asked as she smacked on the bubble gum that she was chewing.

Harmony closed the folder that sat in front of her. "A few things that states you got me and this whole establishment fucked up." Harmony had to get on her boss shit immediately because Renee's attitude sucked. "When you come to my office, you knock first. Secondly, you spit whatever you have in your mouth out before you even make it to my door. Thirdly, all that attitude you got for no reason at all, leave it outside of this business. I'm not sure what's wrong with you, but I remember hiring you and not your attitude, so I suggest you fix it or I will have no other choice but to let you go."

Renee stood there with her nose tooted up and a nasty look on her face. She had her arms folded across her chest and she stood with the majority of her weight on her left leg.

"I ain't got no attitude," she finally spoke after getting read to filth by her boss.

"It really does seem like it. Moving on to more important things. Where were you when I came in? Crystal was here and Jasmin stated that she was on break, so where were you?"

Renee patted her hair to scratch it, to refrain from messing it up. She blew a bubble and it made a loud pop. Harmony winced from the sound.

"I had something to do, but I'm here now. So, why you trippin'?"

This trick done lost her mind, Harmony thought.

"You know what, Renee. Take the rest of the day off and, when you're ready to work and be professional, then you let me know and I might have a job for you. You may leave now," Harmony finished her statement and pointed towards the door.

Renee's mouth fell wide open. Harmony could tell by the look on her face that she wasn't expecting that. She eyed her for a few seconds, to see if she wanted to do more than lose her job for a moment. Harmony had kicked off her black Christian Louboutin pumps under her desk, just in case Renee wanted to go a few rounds with her.

"*Wooooowwwww.* You really on one today." Renee shook her head and attempted to walk out of the office.

"Your attitude is really on one today. Now, you enjoy your weekend and the next few free weeks that you will have." Harmony placed her hands in one another and folded them on the desk. She gave Renee a pleasant look when she glanced back at her.

Renee walked out of the office without closing the door. Harmony swiveled back in her chair and got up. She walked to close her door and Jasmin stopped her.

"Is everything okay?" she asked.

"Everything is swell Jasmin. Thank you for asking, but I see that you have some customers to tend to."

Harmony gave her a warm smile and then closed her office door. She went back to sit down and she grabbed her cellphone to text Chaos.

Harmony: *I just had to fire Renee. Her attitude suck!*

She sat her cellphone back down and continued to work. About an hour or so later, she finally got a response from Chaos. She rolled her eyes when she saw his name pop up, but she read the text message anyway.

Chaos: *Damn. I knew she would be out of there sooner or later. A bad attitude is bad for business.*

She couldn't help but to smile at his text message. No matter what, he always understood Harmony and would tell her if she was wrong or not. She loved the fact that he was in business as well, so he knew exactly what would help her succeed or fail and she always listened to him.

Harmony didn't text back right away because she had to finish up making the last of the orders for her boutique. She was almost done when her stomach started to growl. It was only 1:45 p.m., but then she remembered she didn't have any breakfast that morning. She finished up everything she needed to do, as well as put the order in for the new inventory and stepped away from her desk. She put her pumps back on, grabbed her cellphone and bag, and left out of her office.

"Hey Crystal. I'm going to grab a bite to eat. I'll be back in before closing but, if anyone needs me sooner, just give me a call."

"Okay, enjoy the rest of your day Mrs. Winfield," Crystal said.

Jasmin was busy with customers, so Harmony didn't get a chance to say anything to her. She knew that Crystal was her set of eyes if anything went wrong, so she wasn't too worried about not letting Jasmin know that she would be absent for the remainder of the day.

Harmony hit the unlock button on her keypad and got in. She threw her bag in the passenger seat and put her cellphone on the charger and sat it in the middle console. She put the key in the ignition and started up her car and pulled off.

"Fuck!" she cursed as she ran straight into a red light. Harmony became more aggravated than she was when she left her office. Her stomach was growling times ten and all she could think about was the spicy grilled chicken salad and strawberry lemonade drink from Wendy's. The food was calling her name and the red light was interfering with it. When the light finally turned green, she pressed on the gas and sped off. She made a sharp right turn and tried her best to avoid traffic until she made it to her destination a few minutes later.

21

She was relieved to see that she was only behind two cars when she got to Wendy's. As she waited in the drive-thru line, she let down her window to allow some of the cool air to come in. It was February 11th and the weather had been breezy since the beginning of the year. When it was her turn to order, she pulled up to the speaker.

"Welcome to Wendy's, would you like to try our new pulled pork sandwich today?"

Harmony frowned upon the mention of pork. She didn't eat pork and the last time she did eat it was six years ago. Once she got with Chaos, he cut all that shit out.

"No, thank you. I'll just take the grilled spicy chicken salad with Italian dressing and give me a large strawberry lemonade drink. That will be all."

"Okay, your total is $9.75; please pull up to the first window."

Harmony drove off and pulled up to the window. She gave the woman her money and waited for her change.

"Here you go."

"Thanks."

Harmony pulled up to the second window and got her food. She checked her bag to make sure they had her order right because she was in no mood to go at it with a bitch over a simple order. She ate her food while she tried to find a destination. Not wanting to go home right at that moment, Harmony knew exactly where to go. Harmony pulled onto Landis Avenue and chowed down on her food until she came across her stop. She looked at the time and it was 2:25 p.m. when she pulled into Centerfolds strip club. It was only the afternoon and the scene was packed.

"Lawd, I hope none of these bitches try me today."

Harmony parked and shut off her car. She took a long swig of her juice before sitting it back in the cup holder and getting out.

Beep. Beep.

Her car made a sound when she locked it. There was a semi-crowd outside and all eyes were on her. Harmony's hair blew in the wind and she was looking gorgeous in her black, Burberry v-neck dress and black Christian Louboutin pumps. She wasn't too fond of the stares she was getting because it was hard to tell at times if it was love or hate, and she didn't have time to be guessing.

"Hey Coroner," Harmony greeted the bouncer.

Coroner was the bouncer and bodyguard for Chaos. Not that he needed it but, when he was at the club, people liked to test him and it was always business and money with him. All the other bullshit was simply unnecessary and he didn't have time for it. Coroner was known to put niggas six feet under. He had a bald head with a Sunni beard and he was a big, black, six foot six nigga that weighed a good 275 pounds. There was no busting a nigga head to the white meat or putting him in the hospital. It was putting two in a nigga head and dumping his body so that his loved ones could find him. Depending on the situation, sometimes Coroner got grimy and dirty and wouldn't even leave anything to be found. No one crossed him and, if they did, they would have to suffer the consequences.

"Hey beautiful. It's busy in there. Just giving you a heads up."

Harmony smiled because Coroner was six foot four and he was big and black. He always carried the meanest scowl on his face, along with that try me look but, when it came to Harmony, he had nothing but love and respect for her. He never smiled, but his mean mug softened up when she came around and she couldn't do anything but respect it.

"I talked to Chaos about an hour ago and I see he wasn't lying. I'ma just go in here and check him for a few."

Coroner let her through and she went into the club. She walked through the dark hallway until she entered the dance room. It was nothing but ass shaking and pussies popping. The bar was packed and the tables were full. Harmony was glad to see that business was booming and so early at that. She waved to a few of the ladies that always spoke to her and she gave a simple nod to the rest. She went to the back and walked down the second hallway that led her to Chao's office. Harmony could tell that his office was packed as well, just by the loud noise that was coming from the other side. She didn't bother to knock because she was his woman, so she just grabbed the knob and walked in.

A strong scent of weed hit her nose when she walked in, and she waved her hand back and forth to remove the smoke out of her face.

"Oh, wassup sis," Brave, Chaos' right hand man, greeted her.

"Wassup bro." She hugged him.

Chaos was counting money when he looked up and flirted with her with his eyes. She already knew how he was feeling, once she saw the Hennessy bottle on his desk. It was a few of his other boys there that didn't really matter to her because she wasn't around them as much as she was around Brave. She moved past the few guys that were in her way and went and stood by her man.

"You drinking kind of early," she said, rubbing the back of his head.

"I'ma check yawl later." He pointed to everyone but Brave.

That was their cue to dismiss themselves from his office. When his office was empty from everyone except Brave, he turned his chair around to face her.

"What you doing here?" he slurred just a bit.

Harmony turned her head and looked at Brave. "Can you excuse us for a second?"

Brave swallowed the last of the Hennessy that was in his cup and nodded his head. "Not a problem, sis. Yo bro, hit my line if you need anything. I'ma go out here and keep track of this paper." He leaned over and gave Chaos some dap.

"You already know, bro," Chaos said.

Harmony placed her bag on the empty chair and went and locked the door. "You didn't say anything in response to what I said to you." She took a seat.

Chaos poured himself another drink and gulped it down. "I heard what you said. I didn't think I needed to respond to it because I do what I please. Besides, I'm not drunk. I just got a little buzz. But, you didn't answer my question either."

Harmony crossed her left leg over the other. "And what was that?"

"Don't play with me. What are you doing here?"

"I was hungry, so I decided to get a bite to eat and I thought about you, so I stopped by. I didn't know I needed a reason to stop by my man's place of business and see him."

Chaos stood up from his chair and walked around his desk. He grabbed a handful of Harmony's hair, pulled her head back, and stuck his tongue in her mouth. Harmony could taste the Hennessy, but she didn't mind. She welcomed his tongue and extra saliva in her mouth. While they were kissing, she reached between his legs and grabbed his dick, which was throbbing something serious in his jeans.

"I know exactly why you came here," Chaos said as he lifted her from the chair. He bent her over on the desk and pulled her dress up, ripping her panties off in the process.

"Oh really? Then, why did I come here?" she asked.

Chaos answered her by pushing his thick his thick nine-and-a-half-inch dick inside of her sugary walls. She gasped as he began to thrust in and out of her with no remorse. His balls slapped against her pussy and, even though it was a bit painful, she couldn't help but to enjoy it.

"Oooooh fuck!" she screamed.

Chaos was digging her out so deep that it felt like his dick was touching her soul. He lifted up her right leg and placed it on the desk, knocking things over. He had one hand on her shoulder and one hand on her waist, while he plowed his dick in and out of her pussy. Juices dripped down Harmony's leg as she reached back with her right arm.

"Nah, move ya fucking hand and take this dick."

"I—I—I can't!"

Harmony's stomach was getting overwhelmed. Chaos was definitely rearranging some organs. She was thankful that the music and base was loud because if anyone would have heard her, they would have probably thought that she was crying out for help. Chaos took his hand off her shoulder and put his on her waist. He pumped fast and hard until he exploded inside of her.

"Urgh!"

Sweat was dripping down both of their foreheads. Harmony slowly dropped her leg from the desk, as Chaos pulled out. Between her legs were sore and she had to hold onto the arm of the chair to keep her balance. Chaos stuffed all the dick that he had been blessed with back in his jeans. He didn't care to wipe off because Harmony was his woman and he wasn't fucking anyone else and neither was she.

"You really need to stop drinking that shit because my pussy pays the price for it." She shook her head at her ripped panties on the floor. She picked them up and put them in her bag and took out her wet wipes that she kept in there. Harmony cleaned herself up and threw the few wipes that she used in the trash.

"Yeah but that shit was good. Don't front." Chaos sat back down at his desk and wiped the sweat off his forehead.

"Whatever nigga." She rolled her eyes but didn't deny the fact that he, indeed, did have some bomb dick and that their little sex session was well needed.

"What you about to do though?" he asked.

Harmony went into the bathroom that was in his office and combed her hair with her fingers. She applied a little bit of lip gloss and came back out.

"I'm going home and then I'll be stopping by the boutique later to make sure everything is good before closing."

Chaos nodded. "Cool. Don't be out too late unless you need to be." He pulled out a cigar and clipped the end before lighting it and pulling on it a few times.

"I know baby. Call me if anything." She walked around and kissed him. "I love you."

"Love you more. Make sure you text me when you get home and when you come from the boutique to let me know you're safe."

Harmony assured Chaos that she would hit him as soon as she got home. She left out of the club and said her goodbyes to Coroner.

Beep. Beep.

She unlocked her car and got in. Harmony made sure she didn't show her frustration around Chaos, but he always ruined the moment because he never would tell Harmony *I love you.* When they first got together, it didn't bother her and she figured, since he lived a hardcore life, that was to be expected but now, six years later, she was still getting the same thing and she didn't like it one bit.

She started up the car and pulled off. With a wet ass and pussy, Harmony was deep in thought and, times like this, she wished she had a best friend to go talk to. She didn't have any friends and barely any family. She was an only child and her mother stopped talking to her when she got with Chaos.

"You got so much going for yourself and you rather be with a no good thug. You better not bear a child by him because I tell you now. I'm not claiming those bastards," her mother, Mahogany, once said.

Harmony erased the sensitive flash back from her mind. She wished that her mother saw the man that Chaos was today and not judge him solely by his past. She could admit that Chaos was rough around the edges when they first met. He was in the streets heavy but, as she got to know him and the more she was around him, she learned a lot. Harmony never judged Chaos and, for that, he shared his most inner and deepest darkest secrets with her.

She knew the man that others wished they knew or never got the chance to know. Harmony stuck by his side and they were like Bonnie and Clyde. They started their businesses together and planned to grow old with one another, but she couldn't allow for Chaos to keep giving her half of him when it came to loving her.

Chapter Two

Chaos Miller was a thug and wasn't afraid to show it. He knew where he came from and what he had to do in order to get where he was today and he never forgot that. Chaos remained humble, but he never let anyone throw his past in his face and he wasn't about to start now. He trusted no one but Harmony, his right hand man Brave, and his bodyguard Coroner. Back when he was hustling and in the streets deep, he witnessed many situations as to why a person should never give all their trust to anyone. Loyalty meant nothing if you didn't live by it and, for those who did, he took serious.

Ring. Ring. Ring.

Chaos cracked his eye open as he felt for his cellphone on the nightstand beside him. When he finally grabbed it, he brought it to his face, but it wasn't the phone that was ringing.

"Shit!" he mumbled, reaching for the house phone that sat on the same stand.

No one really called the house phone unless they couldn't reach neither him nor Harmony on their cellphones, which was rare, so he knew that it could only be one hardheaded person that was calling.

"Hello," he groaned.

"Chile, you don't sound happy to hear from me at all."

Chaos became fully awake when he heard his mother, Casey's, voice. He loved her to pieces, but what he didn't love was her calling to wake him up at almost 8 a.m., when he didn't get home until four that morning.

"Mom, why are you calling me so early and why didn't you just call my cell?"

"Because I'm old school. My mother had a house phone when I was growing up. All this electronic stuff ain't for me; now, wake that tail up," she demanded.

Chaos rolled his eyes to the ceiling. He was thankful that he wasn't standing in his mother's presence because after she got done with him, the same eyes he rolled would have been sitting on her kitchen table looking back at him. He sat up on the bed and tried his best not to wake Harmony.

"I'm up mom. Now, what's up?" he wondered.

"It's the 12th and Valentine's day is coming up. I want to go out somewhere nice."

Chaos was a momma's boy and, just like Harmony, he was an only child and there wasn't anything he wouldn't do for his mother. She raised him the best to her ability and no matter how much he ran the streets, she never judged him or gave up on him. Despite the fact that his father died to the same streets, Casey would always tell him the same thing and those words stuck with him for life.

"When God is ready for you to change, you will change. I pray for you every night and put your life in his hands."

"Mom, you don't even know if I have anything planned with Harmony," he said.

"You know good and well that you can do something with me in the morning and spend your evening with your woman. I ain't never been selfish a day in my life and I won't start now."

Chaos scratched his head as he thought about what he could pull together for both Harmony and his mother. "I don't know why yawl women act like Valentine's day is such a big deal. I spoil yawl all day, every day. Shit, Valentine's day is every day for yawl."

"I know you better watch your mouth and act like you know I'm your mother on this phone. Regardless of what you do for me on a daily, I'm talking about Valentine's day. Now, if I don't see you at my door with some chocolates, balloons, and a teddy bear, then problems is something we will have," Casey threatened him.

"Alright mom. I got you. I promise. But, let me get my day started, okay?"

"That's more like it. But, alright, you go on and do what you do. Be safe and I love you more than life itself."

"Love you more, mama."

Click.

Chaos ended the call and threw the cordless phone on the bed before lying back down. It was too early for him to want to do anything, so he snuggled up behind his chocolate drop and wrapped his strong arms around her. He chuckled at Harmony's faint snore. He loved her something serious and there wasn't any other woman that could take her place.

Back when they first got together, he did his dirt, but none of the jump offs he dealt with ever compared to Harmony. She held him down numerous times and she never complained while she did it.

Before he knew it, he had drifted back off to sleep. Two hours later, Harmony removed herself from his grasp. She wanted to smack the shit out of him for coming in late, but she stopped because he already let her know ahead of time so she couldn't be too upset.

"Bastard," she mumbled while flipping him the bird.

Harmony pulled her night gown over her head and let it fall from her hand and hit the floor. She walked into the bathroom and turned on the shower, getting in. She wanted to cook Chaos' breakfast, so she let the water run all over her body for a couple minutes and then washed up. She turned off the shower and got out, wrapping a towel around her body.

She brushed her teeth and pinned her hair up before walking out of the bathroom. Harmony looked through her dresser and fished out a pair of hot pink boy shorts and a black tank top. She knew

Chaos loved the way bright colors looked on her dark skin. She rubbed her body down with lotion and put on her clothes. Just as Harmony was about to put on some deodorant, her phone went off.

Ring. Ring. Ring.

She rushed to answer it before it woke up Chaos. "Hello?"

Harmony didn't even bother to look at the caller ID.

"We need to talk," Renee told her.

Harmony pulled her phone away from her ear and looked at it. She was pissed at herself for not checking to see who was calling before she answered. Renee's attitude was something she didn't feel like dealing with early that morning.

"Renee, are you ever happy?"

She couldn't understand how someone, who was as beautiful as Renee was, could have such a nasty attitude and be miserable all the time. Furthermore, she wasn't sure why Renee was calling her, knowing that she was fired until further notice.

"How can I be happy when you playing with my livelihood? You know damn well that working at your boutique was keeping my bills paid. You gon' fire me but keep those fake ass bitches in your store. Shaking my muthafuckin' head!" Renee being pissed was an understatement.

Harmony took a deep breath before she responded. She was all for a person being themselves, instead of being an ass kisser, but having a ratchet and nasty approach was one thing she didn't allow or tolerate.

"Renee, I warned you back at the office that I am not the one. You really are deep in the wish a nigga woods right about now."

"All I want is my job back and this conversation can be done with."

Harmony put on her deodorant and grabbed her cellphone charger. She put on her slippers and left out of the bedroom quietly. Once the door was closed and she was down the stairs, she let Renee have it, again.

"Now, look, I tried to be nice, but you just keep pushing my fucking buttons, Renee. I fired you because of this exact reason! Your attitude sucks ass and I'm not dealing with it, nor should our customers deal with it. The day you change that reckless ass mouth of yours will be the day you get your job back.

So, with that being said, you have yourself a wonderful day."

Click.

"This bitch gon' have me run dead in her fucking mouth," Harmony talked to herself.

Harmony was always professional. That was one thing Chaos told her that, no matter the situation, always remain professional, but it was hard for her to remain calm in situations like the ones Renee put her in. Harmony didn't like disrespect, but it was one thing to disrespect her and then disrespect her place of business, something she worked so hard for. And, although Chaos gave her the money to start *Love and Harmony Boutique,* it was still hers and she vowed to run a positive business without all the extra bullshit.

She took her charger and plugged it up on the side of the couch. Harmony connected her charger to her phone and laid it down on the arm of the chair. She walked into the kitchen and looked in the freezer and took out some Turkey bacon and Kielbasa sausage. Harmony put the stopper in the sink and ran some hot water. She put the meat in and looked in the cabinet for some table salt and, once she got it, she poured a generous amount in so that the meat could thaw quickly. She looked at the time on the stove and it read 10:35 a.m. Harmony knew that Chaos would be up around 12 p.m., at the latest. He always tried not to sleep in too late because there was business that needed to be handled and money that had to be made.

She went into the living room and turned on some soft music and began to wiggle her slim hips from side to side. Harmony snapped her fingers to the beat and twirled like she was a princess. Looking around the living room as she danced, she realized just how blessed she really was. She had a beautiful home that had three bedrooms and two full bathrooms; a large master suite, fenced in yard, a large deck and central air to top it off. The living room had floor to floor carpet, the kitchen had hardwood floor, and the bathrooms had expensive tile. The vaulted ceilings and remote controlled ceiling fans showed Harmony just how good she was living and she didn't have one complaint about it.

Harmony was so caught up in the music that she didn't even feel Chaos standing behind her, as she was stepping backwards. She bumped into him and turned around, grabbing her chest in a frightened state. She looked up to see him staring down at her with his natural scowl. Harmony quickly went to cut the music off.

"Dammit Chaos! You scared the shit out of me." Her heart was still beating fast.

"You was in ya bag a minute ago," he chuckled, grabbing her chin and kissing her.

Harmony playfully pushed him and went into the kitchen. Chaos was right behind her. He watched her check the meat to see if it had thawed. He slapped her ass hard and watched it jiggle some. Chaos wrapped his arms around her waist and nibbled in her neck. She could feel his dick go from semi-soft to rock hard.

"I don't know why you getting in the mood. Didn't you come in late this morning? Tuh!" Harmony elbowed him.

She was not trying to go there with Chaos at all but, when he grabbed her by the waist and turned her around to face him, she couldn't prevent her pussy from getting wet.

Chaos had a natural mean mug, but he was handsome to the women who enjoyed their men to be ugly-cute. His silky, smooth, umber skin complexion, six-foot-even height, and his jail house built turned the ladies on; especially when he was at the club working. His goatee didn't completely connect or fill in; he had a very thin mustache and a low-cut chin beard. He kept his hair in a low cut and his deep waves could make someone sea sick. Chaos had a serious hardcore look. He had a tattoo on his left forearm of a cross and the date of his dead father.

At thirty-one years old, Chaos took very good care of himself. He worked out whenever he had time and he did his best to keep his stress level down. He tried not to drink a lot and the only drug he dealt with was weed.

"I own that pussy. The fuck you talking about don't get in the mood?" he questioned her.

Although she wanted to drop her boy shorts, bend over on the kitchen sink, and let Chaos beat her walls down; she wouldn't allow it. Harmony wanted to teach him a lesson, and coming in late in the wee hours of the morning deserved some consequences.

"Whatever Chaos, ain't nobody thinking about you. I bet ya ass will know next time you come in late."

"Chill with all the rah rah you talking. I told you before how shit goes for me when the weekend come up. Today Friday, so I'll be getting in late, again. So save all that attitude for when I'm really out here doing some shit. I work, I'm not out here fucking other bitches." He shook his head, walked away from her, and went to the fridge.

Chaos was the CEO of Centerfolds strip club. He was around pussy all day every day, from Monday through Saturday. Not once did he ever cheat or think about cheating on Harmony because she was more than enough woman for him. He couldn't even think of one reason that would make him want to cheat. Harmony had been there with him since he was down and out and just a nickel and dime hustler.

"I work too, but I damn sure make time for you when you want it!" Harmony walked behind him.

Chaos grabbed the jug of White Cran-Peach juice. He sat it on the marble countertop and reached in the cabinet to get himself a glass.

"I really don't feel like going back and forth with you." Chaos poured himself a glass of juice and gulped down half of it.

Urrrrrp!

He belched loudly and sat down at the kitchen table. "You gon' start cooking or nah?"

Harmony rolled her eyes and took out a few of her nonstick frying pans. She made up the pancake batter and buttered up one of the pans, before pouring three dollops in and watching it sizzle. She prepared the Turkey bacon and Kielbasa sausage, along with some eggs and buttered grits. About thirty-minutes later, breakfast was done and it was going on 11 a.m.

Chaos had gone to the living room. Harmony fixed his plate and sat it on the table, along with a fresh glass of juice.

"Chaos, come eat!" she called out. Harmony fixed her plate and sat down at the table. Chaos came in the kitchen and sat down as well.

"Shit look good bae."

Harmony ignored him. She blessed her food and started eating, as if he wasn't there. Chaos chuckled lightly. He thought it was cute when she got an attitude over the smallest things.

"Why you tripping?" he asked while shoving a fork full of eggs and sausage in his mouth.

His taste buds danced around in his mouth when the food touched his tongue. Harmony could cook her ass off and that was one thing Chaos loved about her, amongst her many good qualities. She was beautiful, intelligent, and she could burn in the kitchen.

"I'm not tripping. I'm just tired of having to beg for your time and attention."

It wasn't like Harmony to complain but, lately, Chaos's club had been off the hook. Business for him was always good, but the huge parties and promotion had been spreading like a wild fire. So many people wanted to host a party or event at his club that it kept him busier than usual.

"You never have to beg for my time and attention. I don't know why you acting like that. Besides, I got something real special planned for you. So, just bear with me baby."

Harmony's eyes brightened and a Colgate smile spread across her face. She was so sure that it had something to do with Valentine's Day, and the fact that he brought it up before her made her feel good.

"Something special like what?" She was eager to know what he had planned for her.

Chaos finished eating the rest of his food. He gulped down the last of his juice and got up from the table. Harmony was still waiting on an answer, but he gave none.

"Chaos, are you going to answer me?"

Mwah!

He kissed her on the forehead. "You'll see when the time comes. I gotta get ready for work."

Harmony rolled her eyes and got up. She threw her leftover food in the trash and started to clean up the kitchen. A half hour later, she was finished cleaning and now sitting in the living room with her feet kicked up. Chaos was coming down the stairs smelling and looking good as ever.

He rocked a pair of dark blue jeans and a black t-shirt, with his all-black Jordan sneakers. His black fitted cap and iced out Rolex and rope chain topped it off.

Harmony wanted to fuck him right then and there, but that would only make him late for work and she didn't want to do that. Although it wouldn't matter because he was the boss, but she wanted him to get there on time, so he could come home early.

"Damn daddy." She flirted with her eyes.

She got up from the couch and walked over to him, dusting the invisible lint off. When she was done, she placed her hands on the side of his face and kissed him. They tongue wrestled with one another and, the more they did, she could feel Chaos' dick get hard.

"Let me stop," she laughed.

"Shit, we just getting started." Chaos had a handful of her ass with his right hand.

Harmony lightly pushed him back. "Boy, if you don't stop. If you get in early tonight, then you can do whatever you want to this kitty."

Chaos bit his bottom lip as he gazed at her. "A'ight, that's a plan. I'ma def' try to get in at a reasonable hour."

Harmony was pleased to hear that. They kissed once more before she walked him out and made sure he got in his car safe. She blew him another kiss, as he pulled out of the driveway in his 2015 white Chrysler 300.

Both Harmony and Chaos had enough money to buy all the vehicles they wanted, but they didn't like to be too flashy. Because where they came from, the majority of their kind hated on another's success and they didn't want to cause any unwanted attention. So, they were good with having one car each.

Harmony went upstairs to shower and get ready for work. By the time she got done, it was 12:55 p.m. She was dressed in some green, army fatigue pants that scrunched up at the bottom, black Steve Madden pointed pumps, and a black, faux-leather, sleeveless Peplum top. She grabbed her French Grey Tory Burch bag and locked up the house on her way out.

Chapter Three

Harmony made it to work by 1:15 p.m. She lived on Wilderness Drive in Vineland, New Jersey, which was right outside of Bridgeton. Her boutique was in Bridgeton, New Jersey on East Commerce street. It only took her about twenty minutes to get to work and, on a good day, it took her about fifteen.

She walked into her boutique and greeted Jasmin, whom she saw first at the register.

"Good afternoon, Jasmin."

"Good afternoon Mrs. Winfield. How are you today?" she asked.

"I'm great and yourself? Do I have any messages?"

Jasmin picked up a few cards that she wrote down the call back numbers on and gave them to Harmony. "I'm just dandy! And yes, you have four messages and four missed calls. Here are the names and numbers."

Harmony took the cards and smiled at Jasmin. She was thirty-five years old and full of joy and happiness. Harmony wished to make it to her age and still be just as excited about life.

Jasmin had an anomalous type of beauty to her. Standing at a mere 5'7", her skin complexion was the color of the inside of an almond. She had plump, high cheek bones that she wore Dior Blush Vibrant Colour Powder Blush, 889 New Red on all the time, and big poppy eyes. Her smile was radiant and she always showed all thirty-two. She wore her natural curly hair in a big afro. Jasmin was slim but thick for her size. She was 115 pounds with the measurements of 34-22-40. Her 34 B cups didn't sit up perfectly like the super models or video vixens, but that didn't matter because everything about her body was natural.

"Thank you, and I'm glad you're swell. I see Crystal is helping a few customers and it seems like I'm holding the line up," she laughed. "I'll be in my office. Oh, by the way, the new arrivals will be here this upcoming Monday."

Jasmin gave her a simple head nod and smile before Harmony walked away.

"New arrivals coming Monday, Crystal," Harmony said on her way to her office.

She put down her bag, kicked off her pumps, and sat down at her desk. Harmony immediately got on the phone.

Ring. Ring. Ring.

She tapped her freshly manicured nails on the desk until someone answered.

"Tom Ford's, this is Rachel speaking."

"Hello Rachel, this is Harmony Winfield. Someone gave me a call earlier, but I wasn't in," she said.

"Oh, yes, Mrs. Winfield, thank you for giving us a call back. Are you still interested in collaborating on a design with Mr. Ford? I know, before, we discussed having a meeting and you needed some time to think on it."

Harmony was honored to have such an opportunity, but she still didn't know if she wanted to take the offer or not. She enjoyed being solo dolo, but working with Tom Ford was a once in a lifetime thing.

"I have been thinking about it. But, I just need to discuss it with my husband, and I haven't had the chance to because we've both been working like crazy. How about this? Give me another week and I'll have a decision for you then."

"Sounds good to me, Mrs. Winfield," Rachel agreed.

"Thank you so much, Rachel. Have a great day."

"You too." Rachel ended the call.

Click.

Harmony made a few more phone calls and then started on some paperwork. She was thinking about expanding her boutique in different parts of Jersey. The first spots would be Hopewell, Millville, and Vineland. Everyone loved her dress, heels, and jeans designs and she knew that she would make a killing if she expanded. Harmony wasn't stuck up though. She remembered where she came from. She made sure that most of her prices were affordable.

Crash!

"Aahhh!"

Harmony jumped when she heard the sounds of glass shattering and the screams of her customers.

Her first thoughts were that someone had shot up her business. She got up and ran out of her office.

"Is everyone okay?" she asked.

The customers nodded, but a few of them were shaken up. Crystal ran over and picked up the brick that was thrown through the window. Jasmin walked from behind the counter and stood beside her.

"Wow. Harmony, you need to see this," Jasmin said.

Harmony rushed to their side and grabbed the piece of paper they held. She shook her head from side to side with flared nostrils, as she read the six letter sentence.

I want my job back bitch!

The thoughts that were running through her mind was pure evil.

"I truly apologize to everyone for this. I ask that you all quickly make your purchases. Crystal, Jasmin, you both take the rest of the day off once you ring these ladies up. The boutique will be closed until I get this window fixed," Harmony explained.

"Do you need us for anything?" Jasmin asked.

Harmony shook her head no. "Thank you, but no thank you. I just need you two to finish up and get going. You both will be on paid leave, just until I get the store back in order."

Both Jasmin and Crystal did as they were told, while Harmony went back into her office. She took out her cell and wasted no time calling Chaos.

Ring. Ring.

"What it do gorgeous?" Chaos answered on the second ring.

"I need you to get to the boutique now!"

Hearing the seriousness in Harmony's voice made Chaos drop everything. "Yo Brave, hold the spot down."

He grabbed his car keys and left out of the office. Chaos was damn near running through the club, which made everyone curious and worried at the same time. Coroner stopped him in his tracks.

"Everything okay boss?"

"Something's wrong with Harmony," Chaos said, running to his car.

Coroner knew what his job was at the club, but Chaos was his brother, not by blood but that couldn't make them any closer. He looked at Harmony like his baby sister so, if she had a problem, so did he. He took off and hopped in the car before Chaos could pull off. There was a strong possibility that Renee was not getting her job back, probably not now or not ever.

Chapter Four

"So, you mean to tell me shorty threw a brick through the store window, all because she wants her job back? Shits not adding up ma," Chaos said as he paced the floor of Harmony's office. He couldn't understand anyone who would fight that hard for a job, when they could just find another one.

"Look Chaos, I'm just telling you what she's been saying. I didn't know firing her would cause all this bullshit. But, all I know is it's no longer business. It's personal now."

Harmony didn't want to talk. All she wanted to do was put hands and feet on Renee for the bullshit stunt she pulled. She worked too hard and she wasn't going to let someone like Renee tear down everything she'd built.

She'd met Renee a year ago and, even when she first met her, she was skeptical in hiring her. But

Chaos was all for giving people chances, so she gave her one. Low and behold, Harmony regretted it since that day.

"Chill ma. I honestly don't think shorty means any harm. Believe-"

"What the fuck do you mean you don't think she means any harm!" Harmony cut him off. She was pissed to the max and the more she felt like Chaos was defending what Renee did, the more aggravated she got.

Harmony wondered was there some secret love affair Chaos had going on with Renee that she didn't know about.

"You fucking her or something? Because right now, you being captain save a hoe and I don't like it one bit," she stated, folding her arms across her chest and pursing her lips.

Chaos felt disrespected. His face was contorted in a scowl that was worse than the one he wore on a daily basis. "Did you really just ask me some stupid shit like that?" He stopped pacing the floor and walked over to where she was seated, behind her desk.

"I'm just saying, you protecting her an-"

Chaos cut her off in mid-sentence. "You ain't just saying shit. Baby girl, if I wanted to fuck a bitch on you, I would do so. I don't know how many times I gotta tell you none of these bitches mean shit to me. I'm around pussy every day, so why the fuck would I come seek a bitch from your establishment? Furthermore, ain't nobody protecting her. I'm just saying this shit don't add up."

Harmony didn't say another word. Chaos shut her down in a matter of seconds. She couldn't understand why she would even assume that he would cheat on her, let alone with someone at her job.

"I'm sorry bae. I didn't mean it like that. It's just this shit got me so stressed out. I don't need or want anyone thinking that my business ain't professional. It was customers here and everything."

Chaos looked over at Coroner, who was standing in the doorway of Harmony's office with his arms folded across his chest.

"Call Armando and tell him I need him a favor asap."

"No problem, boss," Coroner said as he pulled out his cell and made the call.

Armando was a Spanish guy that was good with his hands. Chaos had him on the payroll as well as many others. He knew that he could get the job done. Chaos called him whenever shit got real at the club and it needed fixing. Armando never disappointed.

He looked back at Harmony. "Don't let this small situation stress you out, ma. Shit like this comes with the territory of being a successful black businesswoman."

"So, you expect me to just sit back and not be bothered?"

Chaos walked around the desk and grabbed her by the hand to stand her up. "That's exactly what I want you to do. You wanna know another reason why I gave you my last name?" he asked.

Chaos hadn't even told her yet and she was already blushing. "What's the reason?"

He rubbed the side of her face and gave her a peck on the lips. "Because you a lioness. Back in the day, when I was on my bullshit, you was prepared for every little thing that came our way. So, this right here ain't shit compared to the type of shit you dealt with back then."

Harmony's heart melted. It was the simplest words he spoke that came off so powerful. Chaos' love for Harmony ran deep, although sometimes it was difficult for her to tell because he spent so much time at work. With each day that passed, she fell more and more in love with him.

"You always know exactly what to say to make me smile," she told him.

"My job is to keep you smiling at all times, but what I spoke was some real shit from the heart."

Harmony moved in for a kiss but, before she could even touch her man's lips, Coroner came strolling in.

"Armando is on his way, boss."

"I knew he would be. See what happens when you surround yaself with people on the same mission as you? They make moves and get shit done. Which leads me to my next suggestion."

Harmony could only wonder what else Chaos had up his sleeve. She looked up at him and waited for him to speak.

"I want you to go over to Renee's place and holla at her."

"Fuck no, Chaos!" Harmony's nostrils were flared as she cut him off before he could go any further.

Chaos raised his right eye brow at her. He let her hand go and rubbed his together, as if he was warming up. "Who you talking to like that?" he asked as calm as can be.

Before Harmony had a chance to answer, he took a step forward. He was so close to her that as he looked down at her, he could see the sweat forming on her top lip.

"The tone of your voice was too fucking loud and it was very disrespectful. I'm not some bum ass nigga that's around here sitting on his ass. I'ma boss!" Chaos slapped his hand against his chest hard as he spoke.

Harmony took a step back and folded her arms across her chest. She tried to act like she had an attitude and wasn't fazed one bit by Chaos' words and demeanor, but Chaos could see different.

He knew her like the back of his hand so, no matter how she acted on the outside, he knew exactly how she was feeling on the inside.

"Do me a favor and keep that in mind the next time you think about raising your voice at me like I'ma child."

Coroner stood in the doorway of Harmony's office. He didn't want to intrude and make Harmony feel embarrassed by getting checked while he was standing there, so he went out front to wait for Armando's arrival.

"I wasn't trying to be disrespectful. I just don't want any dealings with that girl. I mean, look what she did to my store, Chaos? This shit took hard work and dedication, and I refuse to just let some hood rat ass bitch tear it apart."

Chaos frowned. He understood where Harmony was coming from, but the way she delivered it was distasteful. "I done see a lot of shit in my life and I done been around a lot of grimy niggas and bitches. This girl, Renee, coming at you hard over a fucking job don't seem a bit weird to you? You know people lash out when they want your attention or when they're crying out for help. It's not right but it's life," he explained.

Harmony still wasn't letting up. Her bottom lip was poked out and she was now pouting. That was one of Harmony's flaws. She always assumed without knowing facts.

Chaos didn't mind because he knew he could teach her a thing or two about life. They had been together for a long time and she still had a lot to learn.

"Check it. When your mother wouldn't let you see me back in the day, what did you do?" he asked.

Harmony couldn't help but to chuckle at the childish things she did back then, just so she could see her man.

"What does that have to do with anything?" she asked with a semi-smirk on her face.

"Your lashing out got your mother's attention, didn't it?" Chaos waited for Harmony to respond, but she didn't. "Baby, all I'm saying is to see what's really going on with Renee. You said it yourself. She's a great worker, but her attitude sucks. What person do you know fights for a job like this?"

"Hey boss, Armando is here!" Coroner yelled.

Chaos kissed Harmony on the lips. "Think about what I said," he told her before walking out of her office and going out to greet his worker.

Harmony sat down on her desk and shook her head back and forth. She loved Chaos something serious, but she couldn't deny the fact that she hated how he always saw a positive in every negative situation.

She knew that Chaos felt strong about the suggestion he gave her and she also knew that, if Chaos felt she was in any real danger, Renee wouldn't see another day.

Harmony sighed. "He brought me this far, he wouldn't steer me in the wrong direction now," she thought out loud.

Chapter Five

Not even five minutes later, Harmony found herself sitting in The Jets Projects. She was disgusted at the young girls in their booty shorts and tank tops. The weather was just a bit warm, but it wasn't the type of weather to be dressed half-naked. They were prancing around the young boys and wanna-be hustlers. She shook her head because she couldn't remember a time where she needed to be half dressed to get Chaos or any other man's attention.

"This generation here, boy I tell you," she said as she turned her car off.

Harmony checked her purse to make sure she had her .38 revolver on deck. Another thing Chaos taught her was always be prepared when going in someone else's hood. She looked around for a split second, as she squinted her eyes to see if she could spot Renee's house number.

She turned off the car and got out when she spotted apartment 10. Harmony put her bag over her shoulder and shut her car door. At this point, all eyes were on her and she walked with her head held high as she made her way to Renee's apartment door. Harmony dared someone to jump stupid because she had that thang on her and Chaos was on speed dial.

Knock. Knock. Knock.

Harmony heard kids screaming and running around. The scent of fried chicken hit her nose and made her tummy rumble. Finally, she heard a female's voice and knew that it was Renee.

"Who is it!"

Before Harmony could respond, she heard more yelling. "Sit yawl asses down! I'ma get my belt out in a minute."

Renee slung open the door and was stunned to see who was standing on the other side. The cat definitely had her tongue because she couldn't get a word out. If this was any other time, Harmony would have enjoyed her uncomfortableness but now simply wasn't the time, so she put her pettiness to the side.

"Hello, Renee," Harmony greeted in a nonchalant manner.

"You came here to fight me?" Renee asked. Her attitude was there but not like the usual.

"Fight? Why would I fight you? I actually came here to talk." Harmony's calm demeanor made Renee more nervous than she should have been. That's exactly what Harmony wanted; she was killing her slowly with kindness.

"Look, don't play dumb. I know why you came here. I was just upset earlier and I-"

Harmony put her hand up. "Can we finish this conversation inside?"

Renee was a bit hesitant but, after a few seconds, she decided to let Harmony in. Harmony raised her eye brows at Renee's tiny apartment. When she entered her place, the first thing she stood in was the living room. It was small with a single, two-seater sofa along the wall. Renee's three kids were sitting in the middle of the floor playing with toys and watching TV.

"You can come into the kitchen. I'm just about to finish up this chicken for those monsters in there."

Harmony followed Renee through the living room and into the kitchen. She sat down at the small wooden table. Just by the looks of her apartment,

Harmony could understand why Renee wanted her job back so bad.

"I know you probably wondering why I pulled that stunt earlier," she said as she took out the last of the fried chicken and turned off the hot grease.

"I didn't come here for nothing. Now, tell me what's really going on because a few hours ago, I was this close," Harmony used her pointer finger and her thumb as a demonstration. "To putting this CEO position to the side and bringing that hood chick back to whoop ya ass. But, after talking to my husband, I decided to give you the benefit of the doubt. I wanna know what's really going on."

Harmony was waiting for Renee's explanation although, after seeing her living arrangements, she didn't need one.

Renee stood up against her countertop with her arms folded across her chest. She couldn't front and act like she didn't want to clap back at Harmony like she normally did. But, she knew now just wasn't the time and seeing that Harmony came to her home personally, it showed her that she did have a little bit of care for her.

"I mean, what is there to explain? Look around Harmony. I'm twenty-six years old. I got three kids and a dead beat ass baby daddy. I live in the projects. I got bills to pay and my kids need food and clothes. Oh, and I know what you're probably thinking. If I know he's a dead beat, then why keep having kids by him. Shit, I fell in love with the wrong man, that's why. I'm just trying to make it. I know I got a fucked up attitude, but I'm tired of struggling. I walk to work every day and see those prissy ass bitches in there looking down on me. Nah, they don't say anything, but their actions speak loud enough. I apologize for busting ya boutique window out, but the thought of me losing my job had me going crazy. I did what I had to do in order to get ya attention."

Renee said a mouthful and Harmony listened to every word. She even blinked her eyes a few times to keep the tears from falling. Chaos was right about Renee trying to get Harmony's attention, and she shook her head at the fact that she almost didn't listen to him.

"I can't say that I know what you're going through because I didn't have to struggle as bad as some did. But what I can say is that I can hear the sincerity and hurt in your voice." Harmony looked around for a split second before continuing. "I need two favors from you."

Renee arched her eye brow. "Wassup?"

"The first thing I need is for you and your kids to get ready and meet me in my car." Harmony stood up, pushed her chair in, and headed for the door.

"Harmony, what's the second thing?" Renee stopped her in her tracks.

Harmony looked back at her. "Promise me you will work on your attitude while you're working at my store."

She gave her a wink and walked out of the apartment. Tears rolled down Renee's eyes as the smile she was trying to hide spread across her face. She didn't know what Harmony had planned and she didn't care. All Renee wanted was her job back and she did what she had to do to get it back.

Chapter Six

It was the wee hours of Saturday morning when Chaos finally made it home. When he walked through the door, he found Harmony sound asleep on the couch, which let him know that she tried to wait up for him. He yawned as he walked over to the couch to wake her up.

"Bae, wake up." He shook her gently.

Harmony cracked open her right eye. She took her hand and pushed Chaos away. "So much for getting in at a reasonable hour."

"I'm sorry beautiful, but the club got busy." Chaos threw his keys on the table, picked up Harmony's feet, and plopped down on the couch. He tried to massage her feet, but she kicked him.

"Don't touch me!"

"Come on bae. I said I was sorry. You act like I didn't come home at all."

Harmony reached for her cellphone that was sitting on the coffee table. She checked the time and looked at him.

"Chaos, it's almost six in the morning. You might as well have stayed out and never came the fuck back! I'm tired of your shit!"

Harmony got up and stormed up the stairs. Chaos rubbed his hands over his face in a stressed manner. He was tired and he didn't feel like fussing with Harmony but, considering he was in the wrong, he wanted to fix things before he took it down for the night.

Chaos made his way upstairs and into their bedroom; Harmony was sitting on the bed pouting.

"You mad at me?" he asked a question he already knew the answer to.

"Chaos, don't fuckin' play with me. You know damn well I'm mad at ya black ugly ass!"

He chuckled as he kicked his sneakers off and laid on the bed. "I said I was sorry. Come here." He pulled her close to him.

Harmony tried to push him away, but he didn't allow it. Chaos grabbed her up in his thick arms and laid her beside him as he spooned her from behind.

73

"Chaos, get off me. You do this all the time, then expect me to give you some pussy. Well, not this time."

"I don't want no pussy. Damn! Ya nigga can't just lay here with you?"

"Pssh! Bull fucking shit, nigga! Since when do you ever have the time to just lay with me? Never! So, don't start that fake ass shit now!"

"Wait, first of all, watch how you talking to me. Ya mouth been outta control since yesterday. That's ya only warning. I'm not gon' tell you that shit again."

Chaos got serious real fast and he checked Harmony in a heartbeat. She rolled her eyes, but she didn't give Chaos any back talk. The room went silent for a good five minutes. Chaos was ready to nod off until he remembered Harmony going to check Renee the other day and he wanted to know how it went.

"Bae, how did it go with ole girl from the other day?"

Harmony rolled her eyes once more, as if Chaos could see the attitude she had. As much as she didn't want to talk to Chaos, she couldn't deny the fact that this would be the perfect time to touch basis on a few things.

74

Sighs.

"Babe, she living bad. I mean, I've been to the projects before, but never have I really seen someone struggle like that. She got three kids, and they barely making ends meet. I saw that shit for my own eyes, and it broke me down," she explained.

"You visited the projects before because I lived in them. You ain't never lived that life baby. But, in all honesty, I'm glad you didn't look down on her," he responded as he rubbed her thigh.

Chaos grew up in the projects and he could remember many nights where he went without food. There were times when he didn't know when his next meal was coming. The brief conversation that him and Harmony was having made him think of the time where he was fed up with the struggle.

He was sitting on his bed that was located on the floor of his bedroom. Sixteen-year-old Chaos watched as the lamp, with no shade, dimmed on the wall as the roaches raced back and forth.

Brave, who was like a brother to him, sat right beside him. He was there through every struggle Chaos had since they met and that was over a year ago.

"This shit gotta stop, bruh. I'm tired of watching my mother work all these fuckin' hours for these white folks and getting' paid minimum wage. She's worth way more than that. Hell, we're worth way more than that. I can't keep watching her struggle."

Brave nodded his head up and down. "I feel you, bruh."

"Nah, man, fareal. I'm dead serious bruh; we gotta do somethin' and do somethin' fast. I can't go another day or night like this."

The sixteen and seventeen-year-old sat in silence as they thought of their next move.

"Let's hit the block, bruh. That's our only way to some fast money," Brave told him.

Chaos looked over at Brave. He spoke the words that he was thinking. For a moment, he didn't know what to say. His father had died living life in the fast lane but, right now, he felt like he had no other choice.

"You live by the gun. You gon' die by the gun. We in this together, right?"

Brave made a fist and stuck it out. "We all we got. I'm in this til my casket drop."

After those words were spoken between two brothers that were bonded by heart and not by blood, it was the very last time Chaos and Brave went without.

"Chaos, are you listening to me?" Harmony snapped him out of his train of thought.

"Huh? My bad bae. What was you saying?"

"Well, damn! I see I can't even keep your attention anymore. Fuck it," Harmony blew loudly.

"Chill the fuck out. My mind was somewhere else. Continue the conversation tho'."

"Why? It ain't like you gon' listen. Who was you thinking about anyway?" Harmony was shocked at her damn self for the jealous tantrum she was giving.

Chao removed his hand from her thigh and sat up. He was drained and tired all in one, but Harmony's mouth and actions were out of control, so he had to check her.

"Harmony, get up and look at me," he demanded.

She sat up and folded her arms like a child who had just been told no.

"Who the fuck you think you talkin' to?" Harmony tried to speak, but he cut her off. "Nah, don't say shit. I never have to come at you like this but, lately, you've been gettin' real reckless and I'm not tolerating that shit. Yea, I come home late more than I should, but I'm out here making money. A nigga grew up without shit, so I'm tryna make sure I never have to go without ever again. I wanna know that when I come home, food is always in the fridge and, when I lay my head, I ain't gotta worry about shit gettin' cut off."

Chaos was speaking straight facts and straight from the heart. He couldn't understand why any woman would complain when their man was out making legit money and not out somewhere cheating.

"Chaos, I understand you're out there working, but I work too! You shouldn't have to work as many hours as you do, when I'm bringing in just as much money," Harmony tried to reason with him.

She was getting lonely, which was the very reason as to why she was lashing out. It didn't bother her to come home to an empty house, but what did bother her was spending hours alone, when her husband should have been coming home at a reasonable hour.

"Baby, that's cool for you work. I respect that. Having a business is something good to have up under ya belt, but I refuse to let you be the only bread winner. I came from nothing, and it makes me feel damn good to be able to give the two women in my life everything they need, want, and deserve."

Harmony didn't know what to say. She understood everything Chaos was saying, but that little selfish part of her made her ignore most of it. The money and sex was good, but she needed time and attention.

"Fine Chaos," she sighed. "Anyway, I gave Renee her job back, and I took her and her kids food shopping. You should've saw the look on their faces when I said they could get anything they wanted."

Chaos pulled Harmony close and grabbed the back of her head. His lips met hers and they shared a passionate kiss.

"Shit like that makes me love ya crazy ass more. Do me a favor and just lay with me. No sex, no arguing, just ya body next to mines and the sounds of our heartbeats being the only thing heard throughout the room."

A school girl grin spread across Harmony's face. No matter how many times they had a disagreement, Chaos would always turn things around and say some shit that would have her pussy thumping and her mind gone. She didn't say a word, as Chaos laid down and pulled her close to him. Snuggling up under his chin with her face buried in his neck was all that she wanted.

Chapter Seven

Brave watched Kevin Gates sign off on the agreement for his party at Centerfolds. He knew that Chaos was going to be geeked at the news. He checked the time on his neon-white Bomberg watch and saw that it was going on 1:30 p.m.

Cool, Chaos should be here around two, he thought.

"Aye man. It's good doin' business witcha," Kevin stood up and gave Brave a handshake.

"Oh, you already know it's all good over here. I'm looking forward to this party man; I know its gon' be crazy," Brave said to him.

"You know it man. Tell Chaos to hit me up when he gets the chance. This shit gon' be epic and I need the best of everything, ya heard."

"Straight up, bruh. You know I got you."

Once Kevin Gates and his peoples left the office, Brave sent Chaos a text.

Brave: *Nigga, we got a busy fuckin' week ahead of us. Get yo ass here, asap!*

As soon as Brave sent the text, he heard a bunch of commotion coming from the club. He grabbed his Beretta and ran out of the office. He saw bottles being thrown and the dancers were ducking and running off the stage. Brave ran over, waving his gun back and forth.

"Back the fuck up. Break this shit up!" he yelled in disappointment.

One of the guys tried to get buck, but Brave cocked his shit back. "Nigga, you think I'm playin'? I'll blow ya shit back and wouldn't give two fucks about it. Fuck wit' me if you want to, and ya kids gon' be fatherless."

Everyone was waiting to see the guy bust a move, but he didn't. Chaos was a problem, but everyone knew Brave was trigger happy and didn't give a fuck who caught a hot one.

Security finally got a hold of the situation and they escorted the men that caused the mayhem out. Brave went over to the DJ stand and took the mic.

"The fuck yawl standin' around for? Aye," he snapped his fingers. "Yawl niggas clean this shit up. And to the ladies', yawl get back to work. Ain't nothin' changed."

Brave gave the mic back to the DJ and headed to the back. As he walked by, he shook his head at the two security guards. "Follow me," he ordered.

When they got to the office, Brave took a seat on top of the desk. He didn't even speak yet. Just by his facial expression, the security guards knew they fucked up.

"The fuck is wrong wit' yawl? That shit that took place out there shouldn't even have gone that far."

Big Steve shook his head. "My bad, boss. I was eating lunch when I heard all the commotion."

Ronaldo didn't say anything to defend himself.

"Lunch? Nigga, I don't give a fuck what you was doin'. I'm talkin' about the way them niggas was throwin' bottles and shit. I should've seen you body slammin' a nigga or chokin' somebody. All that weight and height for what? You fat for nothin'!"

Ronaldo chuckled under his breath and Brave frowned his face, as he put his attention on him.

"And just what the fuck are you laughin' at? Ya ass ain't outta hot water, yet. What the fuck were you doin' while that bullshit was happenin'? Oh, let me guess. Back there fuckin' around wit' the dancers. Nigga, we told you before that if you wanna fuck or get sucked on, you gotta pay just like everybody else. Another fuckin' deduction out cho' muthafuckin' paycheck, homie!"

Brave rubbed his hands through his hair before he waved his hand to dismiss the men from his office. He got up and went around his desk to take a seat. He pulled his ashtray close to him and grabbed the blessing that was sitting pretty on the side of it. After grabbing his lighter and striking it a few times, the aroma of some strong ass Loud filled the room and his lungs. He inhaled and exhaled a few times as he leaned back in his swiveled chair.

***

Harmony smiled when she opened her eyes and saw that Chaos was still home. She thought that her temper tantrum from this morning had work, but she was clearly oblivious to the fact he was late for work.

She scooted down and unbuckled his belt buckle and unbuttoned his jeans. Harmony reached in the hole of Chaos' briefs and pulled out his pretty, juicy, thick dick. Not giving the slightest fuck about her morning breath, Harmony began to lick up and down on Chaos' shaft. She slowly massaged his dick with her left hand as she sucked on the head. Pre-cum seeped out as she continuously put her hand and mouth to work.

"Ssss," Chaos hissed as he opened his eyes.

He couldn't even remove the sleep from the corners of his eyes before Harmony deep throated him. Chaos grabbed the back of Harmony's head. She was giving him that sloppy toppy and he was enjoying it until his phone went off again. When Chaos reached for his phone, it lit up and he cleared out the notification. Chaos tried to jump up when he saw that it was almost 2:30 p.m. Seeing his reaction let Harmony know that he was supposed to go to work and he slept in.

Harmony took this as her chance to take even more advantage of the situation. She sat up on the bed on her knees, causing Chaos to reposition to, now, being on his back. She grabbed a handful of his balls and massaged them as she took all nine inches of him in her mouth. She did that back and forth three good times.

"Damn Harmony, fuck!" Chaos' toes curled as his body jerked.

Harmony could feel his dick throbbing and knew he was about to bust. She plopped him out of her mouth and got up, quickly removing her panties and climbing on top of him. She slid down slowly as her walls took grasp of his manhood.

"This dick feels so good baby," she moaned.

Harmony planted both her hands on Chaos' chest and rode him like a cowgirl. He was caught off guard by her domination, but he was loving every bit of it. She grinded her hips, tightened up her walls, and bounced up and down repeatedly. Chaos' eye twitched and his mouth fell open. Harmony thought she even saw drool drip out. His body jerked just like last time, and she hopped off him and began to suck his dick.

"Oh, my, fuckin... da-damn girl," Chaos stuttered as Harmony sucked the cum out of him.

His body started to shake because she continued to suck even after he came. Chaos was drained and out of breath. Harmony released his limp dick out of her mouth and giggled as she watched his chest heave up and down. Her mission was accomplished. She felt like if Chaos was going to leave for work, then she was going to give him something to think about so that he could know exactly what he was missing every time he stayed at work late.

Chapter Eight

Chaos didn't make it to work until almost 3:30pm. After resting up for a few to regain his energy from the bomb ass head and pussy Harmony had thrown on him, he had to get Harmony back by eating her pussy from the front and the back. He had her speaking in tongues and he definitely gave her something to think about while he was gone.

"Where the fuck you been at?" Brave was standing by the front entrance of the club talking to Coroner.

Chaos had a grin on his face as he shut the door to his car and walked towards them. Brave shook his head because he already knew what kept Chaos so long.

"The pussy done had a nigga coming in late," Brave joked as he dapped Chaos up. "Wassup bruh."

"What's good bruh? A nigga done had a long morning and afternoon."

Brave and Coroner laughed. "You seem tired, boss man. You sure you ready for work today?"

"Shit, he better be after the good news I got for his ass," Brave chimed in.

The look Chaos gave let Brave know that he was all ears.

"Look at em'," Brave laughed. "He just inchin' to find out what I'm talkin' about."

"Yo yellow ass always playing," Chaos said and they all fell out in laughter.

"Nah, let me stop. But, we got a big party coming up this upcoming Friday."

Chaos nodded his head up and down. "Okay, cool. Who gon' be the guest of honor?"

Brave took a dramatic pause before he responded, "Kevin Gates!"

That was good news for Chaos and he could see why Brave was pumped up. They always had different celebrities having parties at their spot, but they all brought something different to the table. Some wanted private parties but then others wanted big bashes that brought the whole city out. Chaos was all for more exposure for his business because it brought more customers, more celebrities, and more money.

"Yo, shit gon' be lit as fuck this Friday. We gotta get shit in motion asap," Chaos told them.

"You already know, bruh. So, from now until Friday, we can't take no days off."

Chaos agreed. No matter what, they always took their business serious. They didn't give anyone a reason to speak bad upon them if they didn't have to.

"A'ight, so what we waiting for? Let's get up in here and start setting shit up," Chaos said as he proceeded to walk in the club.

Brave was right behind him, while Coroner stayed behind and did his job as a bouncer. When Chaos got inside, he eyed the scenery to make sure he didn't see anything or anyone out of place. He made it to his office and sat down behind his desk, while Brave shut the door and took a seat afterwards.

"Everything been running smooth so far?" Chaos asked.

"Shit was goin' smooth before that nigga Joe and some other nigga got into it. Some bottles were thrown, as well as a few punches, but me and Carlisa broke that shit up," Brave was referring to his 40. Caliber that he named after the Queen of the Ring rapper 40 Barr's.

"I knew something went on. Niggas was looking real shook when I walked in."

"Yea, they better be scared, and check this. When the shit went down, Big Steve and Ronaldo act like they couldn't control the situation. I was pissed the fuck off. On top of that, Ronaldo back up to his bullshit," Brave explained.

Chaos rubbed his hand down his face. "This nigga gon' end up getting one in his fuckin' head."

Ronaldo was one of the club security guards who couldn't keep his dick out of some of the dancers who would give him a chance. The others ones weren't playing when it came to their job. It was either you pay up front or get the fuck up out their face.

"He's been a problem since we hired him. It's apparent that this muthafucka like fuck our rules and regulations.

"Real shit and that's something I'm not gon' tolerate. You either respect our shit or get fucked up in the process," Chaos' tone was firm and serious.

Brave could see the frustration appear on his homie's face. He didn't want to bring any extra stress to him but, considering they were partners in business, he would've been wrong if he didn't approach Chaos with the situation at hand. Regardless if it was business or personal, they didn't keep anything from one another.

"I feel you, but don't trip because you know we gon' handle that shit. Right now, let's focus on gettin' this party together," Brave assured.

Chaos agreed and took out one of his many party planners. For the next few hours, him and Brave talked and made phone calls to make arrangements for the party. From the busyness of the club and the nonstop running around the him and Brave had to do, Chaos knew that tonight was going to be another long night. He didn't call Harmony and tell her because he knew that it would be yet another argument that he didn't need or want. However, he made a mental note to make everything up to her tomorrow, on Valentine's Day.

Chapter Nine

"What the fuck!" Chaos stormed up the stairs, hopping up two steps at a time into the master bedroom, and looked at Harmony as she laughed hysterically.

Harmony had just thrown a fifth of Henny on him and he was beyond pissed. She took it as a joke because she knew just how to get under his skin and bring him out of character.

"Don't what the fuck me. Who was that bitch texting your phone?" she asked through pursed lips, with her arms folded across her chest.

"Wasn't no bitch texting my phone. The fuck you coming at my neck for anyway? You got niggas coming at you on a daily!"

Harmony waved him off. It was just like Chaos to flip the script on her but, over the years of dealing

with him, Harmony had gotten used to it, so it wasn't as easy for him to get to her as it was before.

"I don't wanna hear that shit. You either gon' tell me who the fuck that bitch is, or I will GPS her number and I'll find out who the fuck she is myself," Harmony warned.

Chaos wiped his hand down his face as he looked at his woman. He knew she was good to pull up on a bitch if need be. He didn't want anyone to get their ass beat over an innocent text message, so he just confessed.

"Baby, it wasn't like that. She's just an old friend who decided to hit me up and see how I was doing. You need to stop fucking tripping. You know you my one and fucking only. Ya guts is the only one's I'm beating down, believe that," Chaos said as he pulled his wife beater over his head and threw it on the floor.

She watched as he unbuckled his jeans and dropped them to his knees, along with his brief boxers. His thick nine-and-a-half-inch anaconda stood at attention. She just knew he was about to punish her pussy by the way it was staring at her.

"The fuck you over there drooling for? You ain't getting none of this good dick after what you done did. I'm about to hop in the tank. As a matter of fact, sit down on the bed and think about what you've done." Chaos headed towards the bathroom doorway before he heard Harmony suck her teeth.

He laughed and went into the bathroom, shutting the door behind him. He knew she was pissed because she couldn't get any dick, but she was just going to have to be mad because he had things to do at the club later. Chaos let the water run over his body for a few before lathering up his wash cloth with some of his AXE body wash. He cleaned himself from head to toe and then rinsed his body. He turned the water off and stepped out of the shower, wrapping a towel around his waist. Chaos wiped the fog off the mirror and admired himself. His fresh line-up he had gotten earlier had him looking like new money. But, that was nothing new because even on his worse day, he looked like a million bucks. Chaos grabbed his toothbrush and toothpaste and quickly brushed his teeth. When he was done, he swished some mouth wash around in his mouth and then spit it out.

"Ahhhh," he made a noise as he stuck out his tongue.

Chaos walked back into the bedroom to find Harmony watching tv.

"Where you going?"

"To the club. Don't ask me a question you already know the answer to."

Harmony rolled her eyes. She watched Chaos drop his towel and expose that pretty chocolate dick of his. The veins were bulging as it stood out at attention. He rubbed Cocoa Butter on his body and then threw on a clean pair of boxer briefs.

"You need to control your dick. That's why those bitches always on you because your dick always hard."

Chaos chuckled. "Kind of explains the way I got you."

Harmony threw the remote control to the side and hopped off the bed. A few steps later, she was standing in back of Chaos, blowing nothing but hot air as she fussed at him.

"Don't say no stupid shit like that nigga! I def' wasn't on your dick like these thirsty, popcorn ass

bitches be. I'm above all. Don't even compare me to them whack ass bitches!"

Chaos smiled inside because he was pushing her buttons and he knew it. *Bet she won't throw shit else on me,* he thought.

"Ssss, ouch!" he winced in pain when Harmony pinched him in his side. It was like she could hear his thoughts. The pinch was followed by a punch in his back.

"Stop fucking hitting me. Then, when I knock your fucking head, off I'll be wrong." He slipped into a pair of red, knee-length basketball shorts with black lining and a black, v-neck t-shirt.

"I wish you would hit me! I wish you would nigga!" she taunted.

Chaos ignored her and put on his white and black Nike socks, along with his black Adidas slippers.

"Why the fuck you got on Nike socks with Adidas?"

Chaos glanced at her. "Because I'm that nigga and I can do that. Anymore fucking questions?"

He wasn't big on following the rules. He always stepped outside of the box and did what other niggas

was afraid to do. Clearly, he was the type that would wear two different brand clothing and not give the slightest fuck about it.

"I guess so but, anyway, what time you gon' be back?" Harmony looked at her cellphone and saw that it was already going on 8:30 p.m.

She couldn't stand when Chaos went to the club, let alone at night time because that's when all the wanna-be thugs would come there and try to act up. Most of all, that's when the bitches got extremely out of pocket because the majority of the ballers came in at night.

"I'm not sure at the moment. You know tonight is Kevin Gates' party, so I gotta get there now to finish puttin' shit together."

"So, why you got on lounging clothes?" she asked.

"Brave already got my outfit at the club. I wanted to go to the club in something comfortable because I gotta finish puttin' shit together, like I just said."

Harmony sighed because she wanted him to stay in with her tonight, but this was one of the biggest parties he'd had, so she had to let him handle his business.

Chaos put on some of his Versace cologne and then turned around to face his lady. He walked up on her and grabbed the sides of her face with his hands in an aggressive but romantic manner.

"You know I love your wild ass, right?" He shared his tongue with her.

Harmony took it with no problem. She loved the taste of him, but her wants caused her to betray him time and time again. "Yeah, I know, but you better get going. The sooner you leave, the quicker you will return."

Chaos gave her another peck on the lips. "Yeah, I hear you." He walked out of the bedroom and she followed behind him. "Give me a chance to peep things and I'll hit you up in a little while."

Harmony handed him his keys to his 2015 all-white Bentley and kissed him once more. "Alright, make sure you do. I love you."

"Love you more." Chaos left out of the house.

Harmony looked out of their bay window and watched as he got in his car and pulled off. She bit her bottom lips, watching his car until the tail light was out of sight. She planned on telling Chaos the

truth that night, but she couldn't muster up the strength to do it.

I'll just do it when he gets back, she thought.

She plopped down on the couch and cuddled up in fetal position, reaching for the remote on the end table and powering on the tv. She settled to watch VH1's hit movie, The Breaks, before dropping the remote by the couch on the floor. Harmony laid down and drifted off to sleep, not realizing she was tired.

An hour later, she was awakened by the ringing of the house phone.

Ring. Ring. Ring

Harmony hadn't even realized she had fallen asleep. She sat up on the couch and wiped the drool from her cheek. She instantly became aggravated because of the loud ringing. It was rare that their house phone rung but, when it did, the noise bothered her.

"Hello!" she yelled into the phone. Her voice cracked from the left over sleep.

"Yo, Harmony, Chaos got shot! I mean, that nigga got shot bad. He bleeding bad. Man, all this shit is bad!" Brave said in a panicked tone.

Harmony's heart dropped into her stomach. She couldn't believe the news she'd just received. At that moment, the room started to spin, her head got dizzy, and her vision became cloudy. Her mouth watered and she swallowed hard to keep the vomit that was forcing its way up, down.

She knew there was a reason she didn't want him to go to the club that night. Her gut told her that something would happened, but she didn't listen. Harmony didn't know that, when she told Chaos she loved him, it would be her last time able to do it.

Chapter Ten

"What the fuck!" Chaos stormed up the stairs, hopping up two steps at a time into the master bedroom, and looked at Harmony as she laughed hysterically.

Harmony had just thrown a fifth of Henny on him and he was beyond pissed. She took it as a joke because she knew just how to get under his skin and bring him out of character.

"Don't what the fuck me. Who was that bitch texting your phone?" she asked through pursed lips, with her arms folded across her chest.

"Wasn't no bitch texting my phone. The fuck you coming at my neck for anyway? You got niggas coming at you on a daily!"

Harmony waved him off. It was just like Chaos to flip the script on her but, over the years of dealing

with him, Harmony had gotten used to it, so it wasn't as easy for him to get to her as it was before.

"I don't wanna hear that shit. You either gon' tell me who the fuck that bitch is, or I will GPS her number and I'll find out who the fuck she is myself," Harmony warned.

Chaos wiped his hand down his face as he looked at his woman. He knew she was good to pull up on a bitch if need be. He didn't want anyone to get their ass beat over an innocent text message, so he just confessed.

"Baby, it wasn't like that. She's just an old friend who decided to hit me up and see how I was doing. You need to stop fucking tripping. You know you my one and fucking only. Ya guts is the only one's I'm beating down, believe that," Chaos said as he pulled his wife beater over his head and threw it on the floor.

She watched as he unbuckled his jeans and dropped them to his knees, along with his brief boxers. His thick nine-and-a-half-inch anaconda stood at attention. She just knew he was about to punish her pussy by the way it was staring at her.

"The fuck you over there drooling for? You ain't getting none of this good dick after what you done did. I'm about to hop in the tank. As a matter of fact, sit down on the bed and think about what you've done." Chaos headed towards the bathroom doorway before he heard Harmony suck her teeth.

He laughed and went into the bathroom, shutting the door behind him. He knew she was pissed because she couldn't get any dick, but she was just going to have to be mad because he had things to do at the club later. Chaos let the water run over his body for a few before lathering up his wash cloth with some of his AXE body wash. He cleaned himself from head to toe and then rinsed his body. He turned the water off and stepped out of the shower, wrapping a towel around his waist. Chaos wiped the fog off the mirror and admired himself. His fresh line-up he had gotten earlier had him looking like new money. But, that was nothing new because even on his worse day, he looked like a million bucks. Chaos grabbed his toothbrush and toothpaste and quickly brushed his teeth. When he was done, he swished some mouth wash around in his mouth and then spit it out.

"Ahhhh," he made a noise as he stuck out his tongue.

Chaos walked back into the bedroom to find Harmony watching tv.

"Where you going?"

"To the club. Don't ask me a question you already know the answer to."

Harmony rolled her eyes. She watched Chaos drop his towel and expose that pretty chocolate dick of his. The veins were bulging as it stood out at attention. He rubbed Cocoa Butter on his body and then threw on a clean pair of boxer briefs.

"You need to control your dick. That's why those bitches always on you because your dick always hard."

Chaos chuckled. "Kind of explains the way I got you."

Harmony threw the remote control to the side and hopped off the bed. A few steps later, she was standing in back of Chaos, blowing nothing but hot air as she fussed at him.

"Don't say no stupid shit like that nigga! I def' wasn't on your dick like these thirsty, popcorn ass

bitches be. I'm above all. Don't even compare me to them whack ass bitches!"

Chaos smiled inside because he was pushing her buttons and he knew it. *Bet she won't throw shit else on me*, he thought.

"Ssss, ouch!" he winced in pain when Harmony pinched him in his side. It was like she could hear his thoughts. The pinch was followed by a punch in his back.

"Stop fucking hitting me. Then, when I knock your fucking head, off I'll be wrong." He slipped into a pair of red, knee-length basketball shorts with black lining and a black, v-neck t-shirt.

"I wish you would hit me! I wish you would nigga!" she taunted.

Chaos ignored her and put on his white and black Nike socks, along with his black Adidas slippers.

"Why the fuck you got on Nike socks with Adidas?"

Chaos glanced at her. "Because I'm that nigga and I can do that. Anymore fucking questions?"

He wasn't big on following the rules. He always stepped outside of the box and did what other niggas

was afraid to do. Clearly, he was the type that would wear two different brand clothing and not give the slightest fuck about it.

"I guess so but, anyway, what time you gon' be back?" Harmony looked at her cellphone and saw that it was already going on 8:30 p.m.

She couldn't stand when Chaos went to the club, let alone at night time because that's when all the wanna-be thugs would come there and try to act up. Most of all, that's when the bitches got extremely out of pocket because the majority of the ballers came in at night.

"I'm not sure at the moment. You know tonight is Kevin Gates' party, so I gotta get there now to finish puttin' shit together."

"So, why you got on lounging clothes?" she asked.

"Brave already got my outfit at the club. I wanted to go to the club in something comfortable because I gotta finish puttin' shit together, like I just said."

Harmony sighed because she wanted him to stay in with her tonight, but this was one of the biggest parties he'd had, so she had to let him handle his business.

Chaos put on some of his Versace cologne and then turned around to face his lady. He walked up on her and grabbed the sides of her face with his hands in an aggressive but romantic manner.

"You know I love your wild ass, right?" He shared his tongue with her.

Harmony took it with no problem. She loved the taste of him, but her wants caused her to betray him time and time again. "Yeah, I know, but you better get going. The sooner you leave, the quicker you will return."

Chaos gave her another peck on the lips. "Yeah, I hear you." He walked out of the bedroom and she followed behind him. "Give me a chance to peep things and I'll hit you up in a little while."

Harmony handed him his keys to his 2015 all-white Bentley and kissed him once more. "Alright, make sure you do. I love you."

"Love you more." Chaos left out of the house.

Harmony looked out of their bay window and watched as he got in his car and pulled off. She bit her bottom lips, watching his car until the tail light was out of sight. She planned on telling Chaos the

truth that night, but she couldn't muster up the strength to do it.

I'll just do it when he gets back, she thought.

She plopped down on the couch and cuddled up in fetal position, reaching for the remote on the end table and powering on the tv. She settled to watch VH1's hit movie, The Breaks, before dropping the remote by the couch on the floor. Harmony laid down and drifted off to sleep, not realizing she was tired.

An hour later, she was awakened by the ringing of the house phone.

Ring. Ring. Ring

Harmony hadn't even realized she had fallen asleep. She sat up on the couch and wiped the drool from her cheek. She instantly became aggravated because of the loud ringing. It was rare that their house phone rung but, when it did, the noise bothered her.

"Hello!" she yelled into the phone. Her voice cracked from the left over sleep.

"Yo, Harmony, Chaos got shot! I mean, that nigga got shot bad. He bleeding bad. Man, all this shit is bad!" Brave said in a panicked tone.

Harmony's heart dropped into her stomach. She couldn't believe the news she'd just received. At that moment, the room started to spin, her head got dizzy, and her vision became cloudy. Her mouth watered and she swallowed hard to keep the vomit that was forcing its way up, down.

She knew there was a reason she didn't want him to go to the club that night. Her gut told her that something would happened, but she didn't listen. Harmony didn't know that, when she told Chaos she loved him, it would be her last time able to do it.

Chapter Eleven

Jasmin didn't get home until 6 p.m. that evening and that was only because she did a little bit of running around before she got home. When she walked in the house, she was immediately disappointed to see that the house wasn't clean. She had been gone since nine that morning and to come home after a long day of work and see her home filthy truly disgusted her.

"Kay, when are you going to start acting like you're the man of the house, instead of one of my children? I can't keep coming home to a dirty house," Jasmin stated.

Her boyfriend got off the couch and grabbed his keys off the coffee table. "I leave your house the way your son leave it. I'm no one's maid around here. Ya son is fuckin' grown, and you should be tellin' his ass to clean this shit up because I, for damn sure, ain't gon' do it."

Jasmin rolled her eyes and threw her keys and purse on the table. She instantly started cleaning up because she wanted to enjoy the rest of her evening.

"Well, it's obvious that you didn't do anything but sit on the damn couch all day," she jabbed.

"I handled business and then I came here. Don't start ya shit girl because I'll leave out this muthafucka and won't come back," he warned.

Jasmin held her tongue on that note. She knew he was serious and he already had his keys in his hand, so he was just waiting for her to slip up.

"Kay, guess what my boss' husband did for her?" she quickly changed the subject.

Kaotic sat down at the table and slouched down a bit in the chair. He really wasn't interested, but he acted as if he was. "Yea and what's that?"

Jasmin rung out the dishrag and began to wipe off the counters. "So, I'm assuming he pulled some bullshit the other day because he came in today with balloons, teddy bears, and chocolates. It was really sweet and I feel like since we didn't do anything yesterday, then that could have been a stunt you pulled to make things better."

Kaotic chuckled. "Ma, have you seen your boss? Shit, if I was that nigga, I would've came there with balloons and shit too. He not tryna fuck that good shit up."

Jasmin gave him another eye roll. "She ain't all that if you ask me, but I get you. In my opinion, Chaos is just kissing ass, so he can continue to do his dirt at the club."

"Ya bug eyed ass sound a little jealous, if you ask me. Harmony bad as shit and ya dumb ass know it. That's why you always come home talkin' shit on her."

Kaotic was just that disrespectful. He didn't give a fuck about Jasmin's feelings, let alone anyone else's. He always said what came to mind and never gave it much thought.

"Whatever Kay. But, I'm off tomorrow, so do you want to do something?" she asked.

"I don't know. I gotta check my schedule, but I'm out." He stood up out the chair and threw up the peace sign, leaving Jasmin standing there alone.

She threw the dishrag in the sink and slumped down in one of the kitchen chairs. Jasmin always put on an act whenever she went to work. She wasn't the giddy person everyone thought she was. In fact, she was miserable and, indeed, she was jealous of Harmony. She couldn't understand how someone so young could have everything she dreamed of and more.

Chapter Twelve

At eleven Tuesday morning, Harmony had just paid her cab fare. Once she paid the fare, she got out of the car and headed in the store. It was no surprise that the store was busy that morning.

"Good morning ladies," she greeted them with a smile.

Of course, she was in a great mood. The dick and tongue Chaos gave her the other night was amazing. Not to mention, she didn't have to worry about him going to work so, once they were finished, she cooked him some food and they cuddled for the remainder of the night.

"Hey dollface." Crystal gave Harmony a big smile, along with a hug, but the difference between their smiles was hers wasn't genuine.

"Hey Harmony. How are you this morning?" Renee asked. She didn't go the extra mile like Crystal did; she felt like she didn't need to, considering she always gave Harmony the real her.

"I'm good honey. I had to come pick up my car this morning, but I also wanted to pop in just to see how things were going. Make sure yawl check the schedules because soon, we are going to open in the afternoon instead of mornings, so we can stay open just a little later. But don't worry, I will be having more workers, so everything won't be on yawl," Harmony explained.

That was music to Renee's ears because she hated waking up early having to go to work. "You don't know how happy that just made me," she laughed.

"I can tell! The way your face beamed when I said it," Harmony said as she laughed as well.

Crystal gave a slight chuckle but nothing more. She went back to tending to the customers, while Harmony and Renee chatted for a few. She had nothing to say considering her side kick was off for the day and she knew damn well Renee wasn't going to sit back and throw any shade.

"It's so hard for me to get up in the a.m. Especially having to get the kids ready for school, on top of me getting ready for work. So, now I'll be able to get up, get the kids ready, and get some more sleep before I come in. Harmony girl, you are a life saver I swear," Renee stated.

"I'm just trying to make sure everyone is comfortable. Mornings aren't my best friend either and I'm working with a few designers, so things are about to get bigger than what they already are."

"I can tell and you know I'm ready for whatever. But, on another note, I do have to talk to you about something," Renee mentioned.

Harmony checked the time on her cell. She didn't want to brush Renee off, but she had to get back home to go over some designs with Chaos.

"Okay, well hold onto whatever you have to say and I promise when I get the time, we can discuss it. I gotta get going, so call me if anything. Yawl have a good day," Harmony said and left out of the store.

Kaotic was heading in the direction of the boutique. He decided, since Jasmin was off, he would come up there and buy her something nice and use her discount. But, when he saw Harmony, he stopped in his tracks.

"Good morning, beautiful." He showed his pearly whites.

Harmony had just opened her car door but stopped to see who was talking to her. The guy didn't look familiar to her, and she intended to just get in her car and pull off, but she didn't want to be rude.

"Good morning, sir," she responded as she got in her car.

Kaotic walked to the driver's side and stood there until she rolled the window down.

"Can I help you with something?" she asked.

"You can start by giving me your number, gorgeous," he said.

Harmony waved him off. "Sorry, but I'm married."

Kaotic couldn't give two fucks if Jesus was her husband. He wanted her number and, regardless if she liked it or not, he was damn sure going to get it.

"Check this. I'm well aware of that nigga Chaos bein' ya husband but, in all honesty baby, he's the least of my worries. I'm tryna get to know you as a friend. I wouldn't mind taking you out to eat and having some good ass conversation; now, like I said, you can start by giving me your number."

Harmony was taken aback by his forwardness. She couldn't believe how turned on she was by the man that stood before her. Although her and Chaos made up, she still was a little bothered by the stunt he pulled on Sunday.

"I like your mentality, but that don't mean I'ma give you my number. I'm very faithful to my husband and I'll be damned if I let six years go down the drain just because you're interested in me," she said with much attitude.

Kaotic laughed because she fucked up and let him in, and she didn't even know it. Just by her keeping up the conversation let him know that she was interested in him and willing to take things further, if the opportunity presented itself.

"Sssss, feisty, I like that. You tryna play hard to get, and shit like that get a nigga dick hard." He reached in her car window, grabbed her hand, and placed it on his bulge.

Harmony felt his thickness and her pussy got wet. She quickly snatched her hand away and started up her car. "I gotta go because you trippin' nigga."

"You ain't going nowhere until you pass off them digits," he stated.

Harmony bit her bottom lip and thought on it for a moment. The brother was fine as wine, and his muscles was busting through his white t-shirt. There wasn't another man that ever caught her eye until now.

A friend won't hurt, she thought.

"Fine, my number is..."

Kaotic stored her number, stuck his head in her window, and kissed her on the lips. Harmony was caught completely off guard but, once she felt the softness of his lips, she didn't deny him the kiss.

"Believe me, baby, there's plenty more where that came from," Kaotic said as he walked away, leaving Harmony in a trance.

She couldn't believe how she just disrespected Chaos behind his back. That was something she never done before and she was disappointed in herself for doing it. It was as if it turned her on for doing the wrong things.

***

Chaos was still in the shower when he heard the bathroom door open and close. His plans were to go over a few designs with Harmony, dick her down, eat some good food, and chill for the remainder of the day. To his surprise, Harmony wanted to start their sex session early because she snatched the shower curtain back and got in. Harmony damn near forced Chaos to open his mouth, so she could stick her tongue in it. He was caught off guard by how dominating and aggressive she was being.

"Damn bae," he managed to slip out in between kisses.

"Mmm, I missed you so much," she said.

Chaos wondered how she could miss him when she wasn't even gone for that long. But, then he smirked and realized he did give her some good ass dick the other night.

Harmony pulled away from Chaos and turned around. She put her foot on the tub and bent over. Her pussy was on fire and yearning to be fucked.

"Fuck me right now, and I mean fuck me long and hard!"

Chaos' dick stood at attention. It turned him on to see Harmony so in control. Sometimes, she teased him, but this time was much different. He grabbed a hold of her waist and slid his dick in her warm pussy.

Harmony gripped his dick with her muscles and began to throw her ass back. Chaos was going crazy and he had to take hold onto the metal bar that was in the shower for balance.

Slap. Slap. Slap.

Between the water and the wetness coming from between Harmony's thighs, the slapping sound echoed throughout the bathroom.

"Harder, baby!"

Chaos let go of the metal bar and grabbed Harmony by the shoulders. He rammed his dick in and out of her as hard as she wanted. Harmony's body jerked violently with each pump he gave her. She began to play with her nipple with her left hand and flicked her clit with her right hand.

"Give me all that dick Chaos! All of it."

After a few more pumps, his body stiffened up a little. Harmony leaned forward, released Chaos' dick out of her love cave, and turned around. Ignoring the water that hit her face, she swallowed half of Chaos' dick and, from that moment, he couldn't hold it any longer.

"Uh, urgh!" Chaos moaned as he released his warm load down Harmony's throat.

Licking and smacking as she gulped down every drop, she made sure she didn't waste any of her man's kids. Chaos couldn't understand where the new attitude came from when she wasn't like that this morning, but he didn't complain one bit. He was too tired to continue to stand, so he quickly washed up and Harmony did the same. They both wrapped towels around each other and then headed into the bedroom.

"Shit, a nigga got a lot of love for you, girl. A nigga don't know what got into you, but I'm lovin' all of that shit," he said as he laid down on the bed.

Harmony giggled as she followed suit and laid on his chest. "You've been working hard and I just felt like you deserve all that I just gave you."

Chaos rubbed her hair softly and then kissed her forehead. "I appreciate it all baby, and I'm glad we got the chance to get a better understanding. This time off was def' needed for the both of us."

"You're right baby, it was. I love you and I'm glad we were able to work things out before they got worse." Harmony looked up at him and gave him a quick peck on the lips.

"Love you more, ma," he responded before closing his eyes.

Harmony released a light sigh. It was mind boggling to her how she could never get an *I love you* from Chaos. However, that wasn't the only thing that had her puzzled. The entire time Chaos was fucking her, she could only imagine Kaotic sexing her like that.

In fact, Chaos had no clue that the wild sex session they had was only because Harmony felt guilty for getting Kaotic's number.

Chapter Thirteen

He kicked up his feet and weed filled cigar and looked around, as he enjoyed the fruit of his labor. Kaotic was a different type of thug. He stood at six foot even, had a delicious Hershey chocolate complexion, a muscular build, and he was tatted to the gods. His waves stayed spinning and his goatee was always trimmed up nicely.

Kaotic was disrespectful, but that's what the women he attracted wanted. He was the type that would be at a stop light and make you suck his dick right there. Through teen and adult years, he carried that I don't give a fuck attitude, and he literally didn't give a fuck. Growing up in and out of group homes and foster homes with no family or stable place to live, he became bitter. He knew nothing about where he came from or even who his parents were. At the age of thirty-one, Kaotic was established the best way he knew how. He didn't have a legit business but getting money was something he mastered in doing.

Whether it was scamming or selling drugs, Kaotic made sure he made a way. The streets were all he knew because they raised him and, regardless of what home he was in, he always ran back to the streets. None of them were his real blood, so he didn't give a fuck how they felt. If he wasn't comfortable, then he was dipping out and it was that simple.

Ring. Ring. Ring.

Kaotic looked at his cellphone ring on his glass table that sat inches away from his recliner. He already knew that it was Jasmin calling him. He shook his head as he reached for his cell.

"Wassup?" he answered.

"Where the fuck are you? Why didn't you come back this morning! Kay, I am so damn tired of this. You come by here and fuck me, but you never want to spend any time with me on my days off!" Jasmin screamed into the phone.

Kaotic pulled the phone away from his ear and looked at it for a moment. Jasmin had him all types of fucked up, and he was definitely about to let her know about herself. He didn't allow anyone to disrespect him and he wasn't about to start.

"Bitch, who the fuck is you talkin' to? You got me fucked up if you think you gon' call me wit' some bullshit. I'm home relaxin' and I ain't come back because I don't feel like being around ya dumb ass, loud ass son!"

The words that spewed from Kaotic's mouth hurt like hell to Jasmin. She couldn't even find the words to say in order for her to defend her son, so she didn't even speak on what he said about him.

"Okay, so what about us spending time together Kaotic? It seems like we fuck when you feel like it and, when I get off work, you just get up and leave." Jasmin's voice was softer now.

Kaotic rolled his eyes to the ceiling. He couldn't care less about the bullshit she was talking about. He didn't give a fuck about spending time with Jasmin, and the only reason he fucked her was because it was something to do when there was nothing to do. Kaotic's attitude was fuck bitches, get money, but he couldn't front and act as if Jasmin didn't catch his eye at one point. That was, until he got to know the real her and he didn't like how she tried to throw her autistic son off on him while she worked. He also didn't like how she tried to be that motherly figure to him and tell him what he should and shouldn't be doing.

"Look, I'll be over there when I can. But, don't call me wit' no bullshit like this again. You got that dumb ass boy over there that don't want to do a damn thing but watch tv and dirty up the damn house. If you want me over there more, then you send that muthafucka wit' his damn daddy!"

Click.

Kaotic ended the call and continued to enjoy his blunt. His mind wandered on Harmony and it made his dick hard. He couldn't wait until he got between them chocolate ass thighs of hers. Regardless of how she played hard to get, he knew he was going to bust her pussy wide open. That was his mission and it was going to be accomplished.

Chapter Fourteen

Two weeks later, Harmony pulled up to the club with Renee looking good as ever. She figured since it was a Saturday and she closed the boutique early, why not go out and have a little fun along with a drink or two? Since she'd given Renee her job back, the two had become mighty close. It was a breath of fresh air for Harmony because she didn't have any female friends. Renee was excited as well for the new found friendship because she finally felt alive and stress free. She wasn't getting into fights or arguing like she did before, when she hung out with the bad crowd from the projects she lived in.

Before they got out the car, Renee pulled Harmony's arm to stop her. "Wait, remember I had to talk to you about something?"

Harmony looked at Renee's hand on her arm and raised her eye brow, causing Renee to move it.

"My bad but, like I said, do you remember that we had to talk? At the boutique, I told you I had something to tell you and you said that when you had time, we will talk. Well, I think now is a good time to talk about it," Renee mentioned.

It took Harmony a few moments to figure out what Renee was talking about but, when she did, she mouthed *oh* silently.

"Okay, so wassup?" she asked.

Sighs.

Renee prepared herself for the tea she was about to spill on both Jasmin and Crystal. "Ya girls ain't right."

Harmony frowned. "What girls?"

"Jasmin and Crystal. Those bitches is scandalous as hell."

Harmony grew uncomfortable. She thought that Renee was actually changing, but it seemed to her that she was trying to stir up some mess.

"I just can't fucking believe you. You just have to find some way to bring drama into the mix, don't you? What is your deal girl? Like what, do you dislike Crystal and Jasmin so much? I've never had a problem out of anyone but you, so how are they scandalous, huh?"

Renee felt disrespected that Harmony would just snap on her the way she did. A part of her didn't even want to tell her what was up, but she genuinely cared about Harmony and, despite her negative out lash at her at the moment, she was still going to let her in on what was going on.

"Both of them bitches was talking mad shit on you. Saying how you high sadity and how you come and go out the boutique as you please. Crystal even said that Chaos was out here cheating on you." Renee shook her head, as if the gossip was about her.

Harmony was surprised at what she was hearing. She didn't know whether Renee was lying or telling the truth. As bad as Harmony wanted to be upset, she couldn't because Chaos warned her that snakes come in all disguises, whether it was business, friendships, or family.

"I'm not about to worry about that bullshit, and you shouldn't either," she said, trying to hide her frustration.

Renee gave her a Kanye shrug.

"Look, all I'm sayin' is to pay close attention to the people who don't clap when you win, and I'ma leave it at that."

Both ladies got out the car and walked up to the packed club. It was March 5th, so everyone and they mama was in Centerfolds. Chaos' club was always packed, but between the hustlers and the people on government assistance on the 1st and the fifteenth, the club made crazy money.

Coroner greeted Harmony with a smile like he always did. "Well, well, well. What brings the boss lady here on this lovely Saturday evening?" he asked.

It was just hitting 6:30 p.m. and the club was bumping. *Freak Hoe* by The Speaker Knockers was playing inside and the fellas that were in the long line behind them was just inching to get inside.

"Hey, it wouldn't be any fun if all I did was work with no play," she responded.

"I can't argue with you there, Queen. Yawl go on in and have a good time." He held his arm out and motioned for them to go in.

Harmony and Renee walked in the club and jammed as they walked away from the entrance.

"Girl, it's crazy in here!" Renee yelled over the music.

It was ass shaking and ballers throwing cash on the stage. The scent of weed and smoke filled their noses as they made their way to the bar.

"Yesssss, honey! This is the spot all day every day!" Harmony yelled back. She waved her hand back and forth, so the bartender could come her way.

"Wassup Harmony, what can I get you?" Candy, who was one of the many bartenders at the club, asked.

"Let me get two jolly ranchers babe," she told her.

"Coming right up!"

While they waited for their drinks, they rocked and sung along to the music that played. Renee was enjoying herself and they had just got there. Since she had kids, she wasn't able to do anything but work. She was so thankful that she finally got on her grown woman and started putting money away for other things, including a baby sitter.

"Here yawl go," Candy said as she slid their drinks towards them.

"Thanks honey, and put our drinks on Chaos' tab. But, this right here is for you." She slid a twenty to Candy.

Although all of Chaos' workers were paid good money, she knew the extra tips would help as well. Everyone had bills to pay and giving someone a little extra when she had it wasn't a problem in her eyes.

"No problem and thanks for this." She gave Harmony a wink.

Harmony took a sip of her drink and watched the dancers shake their ass. She was impressed by how flexible a few of them were.

"Damn, her ass big," Renee said as she frowned.

"Girl, you is stupid, but hey; if that's what makes her money, then so be it. can't knock her hustle," Harmony said.

"Yea, but once that ass deflates, that money is gone!"

Harmony burst into laughter at what Renee had just said. She couldn't front and act like she didn't notice the dancer's large plastic ass. While they cracked jokes and shared good conversation, they both finished their drinks and ordered another round soon after that.

"Yo, yo, yo, it's time for the ladies to take a break and air those asses out. Fellas, in the meantime, yawl go on and head over to the bar. Sip on a lil something and do a lil mingling, ya heaaarrrrd me!" DJ Funny announced after he turned off the music.

The club roared in laughter. Renee sipped her drink and then quickly tapped Harmony. "Girl! Who the hell is that?" she asked as she pointed in his direction.

Harmony looked to where Renee was pointing and laughed. "Oh, that's Brave, the second owner of the club. You want me to introduce him to you?"

Renee's eyes almost popped out of her head because of how wide they got. "Don't play with me, Harmony. Are you serious?"

She couldn't help but to chuckle again at Renee and her actions. It amused her on how Renee thought she was playing when she said she would introduce the two.

"Watch this," Harmony said as she waved in Brave's direction.

He held up his finger, as if to say *one minute*, while he finished talking to one of the workers. A few moments later, Brave finally walked over to where Harmony and Renee was sitting at the bar.

"Wassup sis. Bro already know you here. He in the back if you need me to go get him," he said.

"I know where he is and I'm here enjoying myself. Damn, I can't even sneak in without him scoping me out." She shook her head in fake disappointment.

"Chill wit' all that. You know bro got eyes on you just like the security cameras we got around here," Brave laughed.

Brave was keeping it real. Chaos always had a set of eyes on Harmony, even when they weren't his own, and his club was well planted with security cameras. So, what seemed like a joke to Harmony was clearly Brave being serious and letting her know that she was Chaos' life.

Harmony simply waved him off and got back to the situation at hand. "Brave, I want you to meet a friend of mines." She smiled as she glanced at Renee.

Brave looked surprised because for as long as he'd known Harmony, not once did she have any friends. "Friend? Damn sis, I guess I don't be around enough."

"Boy, shut up," she laughed as she gave him a playful push. "She works at my boutique and she's good peoples. You know I don't fuck with too many. Let alone females, so you know she's good money."

Brave nodded, turned his attention to Renee, and extended his hand. "Wassup gorgeous?"

Renee blushed instantly. All she could do was smile bashfully and sip her drink. She completely ignored the fact that Brave had his hand out. Harmony chuckled at how nervous Renee got when Brave gave her his attention.

This was nothing new to Brave because he always had the females feeling some kind of way when it came to him. He could literally talk the panties off any woman he wanted. Brave stood directly in front of Renee and leaned over so that both his hands were on bar and he was face to face with her.

Renee got hot all over and melted inside, as she tried to keep her composure. The look Brave was giving her made her want to fuck him right then and there.

"So, you just gon' ignore a nigga?"

Harmony smirked and shook her head. She knew that Brave knew that Renee was feeling him. He was messing with her head at the moment and Harmony could just imagine how wet Renee's panties were because she could remember a time when Chaos did her the same way.

"Uh, I mean, no," she fumbled to find the words to say.

"That's what it seems like. I done tried to shake ya hand and introduce myself, and you actin' all shy. I don't bite beautiful," he laughed. "I mean, that's only if you want me to."

It was like love at first sight with Renee, and that was a feeling she never felt before. As many times as she fucked her baby dad, not once did she ever have the feeling that Brave was giving her, and the crazy part about it was that he never even touched her. His scent alone had her mind blown.

Brave licked his pink lips. "So, wassup? You gon' tell me ya name?"

Renee took a sip of her drink and looked Brave up and down. His crinkly dreads hung past his shoulders, and she could tell he had just got finished smoking because his eyes were low and she could smell a strong hint of weed that had stayed on his clothes. But, that still didn't take away of the divine smell that came from him.

"It's Renee," she finally spoke up.

Brave stood up and pulled out his phone, while Renee undressed him with her eyes. He was five-foot-eleven and he had the skin complexion of a cashew peanut. Her eyes couldn't help but to wander downwards and her heart fluttered by the sight of the huge bulge that could be seen through his jeans.

"Chill lil mama. This ain't what you want," he said, noticing where her eyes were looking.

Renee quickly looked away, embarrassed by being caught acting like a pervert.

"You gon' let a nigga get ya number?"

Renee looked over at Harmony, and Harmony looked back at her with a confused look. "Girl, you better stop playin' and give my bro ya number."

She took another look at Brave and then gave him her number; she watched as he programmed it in his phone.

"A'ight sis. I'm bouta get back here and finish handling business."

"Okayy bro," Harmony said as she began to dance to the music DJ Funny put on.

Brave didn't say another word to Renee. All he did was give her a simple head nod before turning away and heading to the back. At that point, Renee didn't know how to feel. She wasn't sure if she had just been played or on her way to getting played by a pretty boy because that's exactly what Brave was. A few moments ago, he was all up on her, and then, just like that, he gave her a head nod as if she was his homeboy.

"What just happened?" Renee asked.

Her tone was a bit childlike. She sounded hurt by Brave's actions, and she wondered did Harmony bring her to the club just to embarrass her because that how she was feeling.

"Um, what do you mean what just happened? You just got Brave's number and you should be happy because he's a good dude."

Renee looked over at Harmony in frustration because she still felt played. "What the hell do you mean I should be happy? Do you see how he just took my number and dipped off? Fuck that, I'm not about to get played by no one!"

She got up and slammed her cup on the bar and stormed out of the club. The drinks started to kick in and Harmony had a slight buzz, but she wasn't fucked up to the point where she didn't know what was going on. Renee was too bothered by the little encounter her and Brave had, and she was going to find out why. Harmony got up and walked out of the club to find Renee. She saw her leaning on her car, so she headed in her direction.

"What was the about? I mean, you really bothered that he gave you a head nod?" Harmony was confused.

Renee had her head down when Harmony walked up. When she looked up, Harmony could see tears in her eyes and that completely knocked her buzz off because she became really concerned.

"Renee, are you okay? I'm fareal now girl, this ain't just about Brave giving you no damn head nod. What's going on?"

She threw her hands up as if to say *I give up.* "Oh, stop the act Harmony. You don't give a fuck about me, and that's why you brought me here. Just to get played!"

141

Renee was mad and hurt all in one. Harmony was beginning to think she had some sort of mental issues because if any woman got mad over a simple head nod, there were definitely some hidden issues that Renee needed help with, and if she and Harmony were going to take their friendship any further, she needed to know what was up.

"Look, I'm not going to waste my God given time to bring you all the way down here, just so you could get your feelings hurt. That's not how I move! We supposed to be out having a good fucking time, and you storming out of clubs and shit. What kind of shit is that Renee? This is some straight young girl shit! Brave is a boss ass nigga and if you can't handle him giving you a simple head nod, then how the fuck do you expect to fuck with him? You way too emotional sweetie," Harmony said.

"I'm not like you, okay? I've been through hell and back with niggas. Especially my kids no good ass father. That nigga fucked me over the entire time we were together. I refuse to go through that again," she whimpered.

Harmony sighed as she ran her fingers through her hair in a stressed manner. She looked around as if someone was watching them, but it was only because she knew that the situation that was playing out before her was going to take some time to fix.

"Like me? You act like shit is perfect in my world. I go through shit too, but it's all about keeping it together. You gotta be a woman on her boss shit out here. If you're going to weep, then do that shit behind closed doors. Never let anyone see you sweat! Not these bitches or these niggas!"

By now, Harmony was in Renee's face. She placed her hand under her chin like a mother would do her child and lifted her head up.

"That stops tonight. All that feeling bad about your past and hating yourself for falling in love with the wrong man stops tonight. You can't change your past, but you damn sure can prevent the same shit from happening in your future."

Renee shook her head *no*. "I can't Harmony. This is who I am. This is all that I'm used to."

Harmony lifted her head once more, when Renee tried to look down. "Nah, fuck that. That shit stops tonight. It doesn't matter what you're used to. It's about what you're going to stop. Life is too short, and sulking in your misery is not what we gon' do. If you plan on being friends with me, then I'ma need for you to step it up. Be a woman with confidence. Love yourself and, regardless of whatever it is that you go through, always make sure you pick yourself up and dust yourself off."

Renee wiped the tears from her face and cleared her throat before she spoke again. "I just thought Brave was an okay guy, but then being all up on me like that and then giving me a head nod like I was some nigga just made me feel like damn, am I good enough to attract a guy like him? That fast, he switched up on me," she explained.

Harmony let go of her face and laughed. "Girl, Brave is just a chill ass dude and, besides, it's only so much bullshittin' around that he do at his place of business." She placed her hand on Renee's shoulder. "Look, just promise me that you will try to enjoy the rest of your night and that you will work on being more confident?"

Renee looked at Harmony and thought on it for a few. She was an emotional wreck, but she couldn't be happier to have Harmony by her side during one of her depressing moments. She could tell that they were starting to get a lot closer and that's exactly what she wanted. Renee appreciated every bit of advice Harmony gave her and she was glad to learn things from her because she loved the woman Harmony was.

"I can't say that it's gon' happen overnight, but I'll damn sure try," she said.

Harmony smiled. "That's all I ask for is that you try honey. Now, can we please get back in this club, so I can have a few more drinks? You done blew a bitch buzz with this shit," she laughed.

Renee laughed along with her. "I'm sorry girl!"

"It's cool. I understand that life is hard and, sometimes, too much to bare, but you will learn soon enough that it's better to move forward, then to constantly look behind you."

Renee shook her head up and down, basically agreeing with Harmony.

"You good? We can go back inside now?" Harmony searched her face for an answer.

Renee smiled big, showing her beautiful set of pearly whites. "I'm good girl."

Harmony threw her hands up to the sky. "Thank God!"

They both shared a laughed as they headed back towards the club. When they got inside, the ladies were back on the stage. Both Harmony and Renee got more than an eyeful and they didn't mind because they were both too busy ordering another round of drinks and continuing their good time.

Chapter Fifteen

It was 10 a.m. Sunday morning. Harmony cracked one eye open and looked around. She had a slight headache and she didn't mind one bit because she had a great time, something she hadn't done in quite a while, due to her always being busy with work, but Harmony had a lot to celebrate. With her working with Tom Ford, her boutique expanding, and her relationship with Chaos was better than ever, Harmony was in a good space. She even had a newfound respect for Renee, and she couldn't wait to get to know her more because she was enjoying the softer side of her, instead of always seeing her with an attitude.

Harmony threw the comforter off her and stretched. She let out a yawn and then she let out a loud fart.

Pwwaarrrrppppp!

"Damn!" Harmony frowned her face at how bad her fart smelled.

"What the fuck Harmony!" Chaos yelled in a groggy tone.

She jumped out of bed, frightened because she had no clue that Chaos was home. His face was frowned up and he was even fanning the smell away, causing Harmony to laugh because from the looks of it, he got the full effect of the smell.

"I'm sorry baby. I didn't even know you were home," she said in an innocent voice.

Chaos looked over at her. "So, this is what you do when I'm not home? Fart loud like that? That shit stink bae, fareal."

Harmony was a little embarrassed. Not because she never farted around Chaos, but because she never let one loose the way she did.

"Boy, no, I don't just fart in the house while you're gone. Anyway, what are you doing here? I thought Saturdays were busy for you?" she asked.

Chaos rubbed the sleep out of his eyes. "I came home around 2:30 and you were knocked out. I was too tired to even wake you up to tell you I was home, so I crashed right along with you. But, after the shit you just pulled, I'll make sure I let you know that I'm here, so I won't have to run into yo funky ass again."

Harmony burst into laughter. "Shut up! Now you see how comfortable I am around you."

Chaos waved her off. "Hell nah. Yo ass was caught off-guard. Don't act like you did that shit before. I mean, maybe I was in the bathroom while you was shittin' but never have you ever done that. I mean, that shit was tragic!"

Chaos was going on and on about Harmony passing gas. He had her cracking the hell up with tears running down her face. It was just like him to take an embarrassing situation for her and make light of it.

"I can't with you right now, ugh!" she laughed. "But anyway, I got a lot to tell you about the other night."

Chaos adjusted the pillow in back of him and laid down. "Come on funky booty. Come lay on daddy's chest and tell me all about it."

Harmony rolled her eyes as she smirked at him. She crawled back into bed and laid right beside him and placed her head on his muscular chest.

"Babe, before I get into my drama. Whatever happened to the Kevin Gates' party? It was supposed to be Friday before last but, yet, I'm still seeing flyers for it and the streets is talking about how lit it's going to be."

"The party got postponed, bae. This shit is gon' be big. This dude want the whole street shut down, and only those who are coming to the party can come down the street where my club at. This nigga spending crazy dough on this party. He got strippers from King of Diamonds performing, and the club is gon' be packed with mad celebrities. This shit gon' be more than lit and that's why we have to postpone, just to make sure everything is straight."

Harmony got excited just by listening to the detail Chaos was giving her. She had met a few celebrities before by going to Chaos' club, but that's not why she was excited. She was happy for her man because his dream finally came true. Having his own business and working with celebrities was something he always talked about back in the day. There had been plenty of times Chaos said that he was going to open up a club and every celebrity was going to want to chill there. Low and behold, he was right, and

Harmony was glad to be right by his side as his dreams came to life.

"Wowww! You do realize we about to blow up, right? I mean, after this party with Kevin Gates and me working with Tom Ford? You know we gonna be the talk of the fuckin' city, and that shit gonna bring more problems," Harmony's tone changed. She worried about Chaos every day because the hate was real where they came from.

"Baby, don't worry about the negative; let's just focus on the blessings that's raining down on us. We deserve everything we're getting because we worked hard for it," he explained.

Harmony didn't respond. She rubbed his chest and listened to his heart beat. She loved that man to the moon and back, and although Chaos told her not to worry, somehow, she still did.

"Why you get so quiet?" he asked, already knowing the answer.

"No reason but, anyway, me and Renee had a serious talk yesterday. I really think she's a cool person. I just wish she stop trying to bash Crystal and Jasmin."

"What you mean bash them?" he repeated.

Harmony sat up and crossed her legs and gave Chaos direct eye contact. "The other night when we pulled up to the club, she said she had to tell me something. So, I asked her what was up, and she told me that Crystal and Jasmin was talking mad shit on me. I had to check her real quick."

Chaos scratched his head. "Why?"

"What do you mean why? I had to because I felt like she was just trying to stir up some mess so that I could fire them or something like that."

"You startin' to slip a lot ma, fareal." Chaos seemed disappointed.

"Huh? How? What did I do wrong, Chaos?"

He wiped his hand down his face in a frustrated manner. Chaos taught Harmony the ins and outs when it came to business and any kind of relationship. It seemed like the more he tried to teach her, the more she took matters into her own hands. If she was just some random person, he would let her find out things the hard way but, considering she was the love of his life, he couldn't see her make stupid mistakes.

"For one, no matter what type of information you receive, you never allow the messenger to see you sweat. That right there is a no, no. Furthermore, I don't know Renee and I don't care to know her, but you ever heard of that saying the loudest one gets ignored?"

Harmony couldn't quite figure out where he was going because she never heard of a saying that went like that.

"Don't look at me like I'm speaking Chinese. I don't exactly know how the saying goes, but I know it basically means no one listens to those who are loud. So, what I'm sayin' is hypothetically speaking, let's say Renee is tellin' the truth. She done pointed out two snakes that you doin' business with but because she's known for having an attitude and being loud, as well as ratchet, you ignore her."

Harmony began to bite her thumb nail as she thought about what Chaos was saying. Once again, he was making a valid point, and she didn't understand why she couldn't figure something out without him having to break it down for her.

"So, you think she's telling the truth?"

Chaos sighed. "I said hypothetically bae, but my thing is, if you don't believe her, you can always go back and watch the footage. Shit, me and Brave make sure we watch the security footage every night, just in case we missed something."

Harmony wanted to smack herself in the face. She wondered why she didn't think of that in the first place. "You right baby. I'ma take out some time next week to go over the footage and see what's up with this situation before I go any further," she assured.

Chaos nodded. "Cool, so what serious talk did you and Renee have?"

"Ooooh, well she was telling me how her kids' father did her and some other shit she'd been through with guys she dealt with in her past." Harmony gave him a brief story because she already talked his head off with the other situation.

Chaos didn't respond, but she could tell he was listening.

"Do you think I should trust her?" she asked.

"I can't tell you who or who not to trust. All I'ma say is go by a person's actions. Talk is cheap, but someone's actions means a lot. She could tell you all of her business and still stick a knife in ya back. This day and age, bitches and niggas tell you just enough to make you feel like yawl bonding. But, come to find out, that was just their way to get close to you. Get you to open up to them, so they can sneak their way in and fuck you over. Now, I'm not sayin' that's what Renee is doin', but always keep ya ears and eyes open. If it don't sit right with you, nine times outta ten, it ain' right ma," Chaos said, getting up off the bed and going into the bathroom, while leaving her thoughts to sink in.

Harmony hated how Chaos left her mind boggled. He would preach to her, and then hit her with a twist that would really have her thinking. She had so much to think about and she didn't want to take anyone on the new journey with her, if they were fucking her over.

***

3 p.m. Sunday afternoon

Brave had just stepped out of the shower. He wrapped his towel around his waist and left out of his bedroom. He walked down the hallway and into the kitchen.

"A nigga starvin' like marvin'," he said out loud.

He looked through the cabinets and refrigerator and shook his head. It was packed with food, but he didn't feel like cooking. All he wanted to do was relax and that's exactly what he intended to do. Brave grabbed a menu off the fridge and went back to the bedroom to get his cellphone. He ordered pizza, wings, garlic bread, and pasta to hold him over for the day.

Once he was finished placing his order, he took his phone and his charger and left out of the bedroom once again. He went down the hallway and into his living room, plopping down on the couch still in his towel. He grabbed the remote control and searched through his DVR until he found the hit show, Empire. He was a fan of the tv series and, at one point, he was a fan of Power. That was until 50 Cent started acting like a bitch. Brave couldn't respect 50 Cent's actions. It was bad enough black people couldn't understand the power they carried and how strong they really were. Then, to have a black man bash another black man and woman just didn't sit well with him; he felt like coming together as one was always better than beefing.

Brave threw the remote beside him and reached on the side of the couch to recline his chair. He unlocked his phone and scrolled through his contacts. When he came across the name he was looking for, he sent a text.

Brave: *Wassup beautiful?*

Renee: *Who is this?*

Brave: *Guess who?*

He laughed because he was about to fuck with her mind for a little, just to kill time until his food came.

Renee: *Who the fuck is this playing on my phone!*

Brave burst into laughter. She got pissed way too easy, and it was funny to him because if she knew who she was talking to, she wouldn't dare be disrespecting him.

Brave: *Relax baby. How about I give you a hint, cool?*

Renee: *Whatever...*

He got preoccupied, so he couldn't respond right away like he'd been doing. Brave was entertained by the episode of Empire and then his food, came which was a win, win to him. After getting up to answer the door and paying for his food, he went into the kitchen to put the food on the stove.

Brave fixed himself a healthy plate, got a cold Pepsi out the fridge, and headed back into the living room to finish enjoying his show. He decided to text Renee back and let her know that it was him playing with her.

Brave: *I thought you would've been Brave enough the other night. Guess you not built like that.*

If he could've witnessed the smile that spread across Renee's face when she received that text message, he would've thought she had won the lottery.

Renee: *Omg! Why are you playing on my phone silly, lol.*

Brave chuckled and decided to mess with her some more because he knew she liked him. He always played with the females' heads. It wasn't anything personal; it was just that he was the player type and he knew what he was capable of. Getting into a female's mind was so easy for him to do, so he did it for fun. Instead of texting her back, he called her.

Ring. Ring.

The phone barely rung twice before she answered. "Hello," she answered seductively.

Brave's dick jumped a little. She was so nervous the other night that he didn't really get a chance to hear what she sounded like.

"What's goin' on wit' you, love?"

"Just sitting here with my kids. How about you?"

Brave frowned at her response. He wasn't too fond of women who had kids because he wasn't ready to play daddy to anyone. He enjoyed being single and he enjoyed fucking women and sending them on their way. He didn't need any tag-a-longs at all.

"Damn, you got kids?" he asked again, as if she didn't already answer the question.

"Yeah, is that a problem?" she asked in defense.

Brave noticed the change of her tone. "I mean, not really. I'm just not the kind of guy that likes to deal with women with kids. Too much baggage, in my opinion."

Renee pulled the phone away from her ear and looked at it. Her first thoughts were to hang up but, for some reason, she felt like getting to know him and showing him that she was different could possibly change his mind in the future.

"As long as the woman takes care of her kids, then it's not baggage at all," she responded once she put the phone back to her ear.

Brave shrugged his shoulders.

"I hear you, but fuck all that though. Last night, I had you speakin' in tongue. So, I'm tryna figure out wassup wit' me and you?"

Renee laughed. "Boy, you did not have me speaking in no damn tongue."

"Watch all that boy shit wit' me, ma. I'ma grown ass man over here, believe that."

"Oh, I, I didn't mean anything by it," she stuttered.

"Yeah, well, next time, watch how you come at me. That lil boy shit don't fly this way," he stated.

An awkward silence took place after Brave put his foot down. Renee just knew she fucked up and she felt like there was no way of her getting the chance to get to know him now. A few minutes passed, and Renee still couldn't find the words to say. She was embarrassed, and it was as if Brave knew that she was.

"Fuck you so quiet for?" he broke the silence.

"I don't know. Seems like I fucked shit up before it got started," she said just above a whisper.

Brave undid the towel, grabbed his dick, and started to play with it. He was horny as shit and it had been a while since he had some pussy, due to him being so busy. He was in the mood for some warm pussy and head, but he was a little hesitant to invite her over because he didn't trust anyone, and bitches were grimy these days.

Although Harmony spoke highly of Renee, Brave could tell that she had some ghetto in her. He was very cautious when it came to hood bitches because they had no filter. They would see a boss ass nigga on their shit and try to take him for everything they had or become a needy bitch. That was something Brave didn't have time for, but he couldn't front and act like he wasn't intrigued on what Renee was about because Harmony didn't fuck with anyone but him, Chaos, and Coroner. He was bound to get close to her and see what the fuck made Harmony choose her as a friend. It would kill him and Chaos if something bad happened to Harmony, due to her bad judge of character.

Fuck it, he thought.

"You feel like comin' through?" he asked.

Renee's mouth fell wide open. She looked at the phone and checked to see if her volume was all the way up, just to make sure she was hearing right.

"You serious?" she asked in a shocked tone.

"I'm dead ass."

Renee was about to accept his offer until she realized she only paid her babysitter Monday through Fridays. Saturday and Sunday was her off days, unless her schedule changed and she doubted that she would be able to get her sitter over at spare of the moment.

"Shit! Brave, I can't. I just remembered I don't have a babysitter for weekends."

"Call ya babysitter. I'll pay her double of what you pay her. See if she can keep the kids overnight and I'll take you to work in the am. Let them know that when you get off work, that's when they will get paid," he told her.

Renee couldn't believe how sweet Brave was being and they didn't even know each other. She wasted no time in letting Brave know that she would text him for the address, after she got off the phone with her sitter.

While Renee was handling business on her end, Brave took it upon himself to put on some clothes. He went down the hall to his bedroom and looked in his dresser for a pair of sweatpants. It was his lounging day and that's all he put on. Five minutes later, he heard his phone go off. He tapped the screen, so it could light up and he could read his notification.

Renee: *Everything is a go. She lives a few apartments down from me, so she just got here. What's your address?*

Brave loved how she didn't waste him time by beating around the bush. He texted her his address and then put his phone down. He ate his food and waited patiently for her arrival.

Knock. Knock. Knock.

Brave jumped out of his sleep. He didn't even realize he'd dosed off, but the knocking on his door woke him straight up. Before he got up to answer the door, he picked up the remote and pressed zero on it, which turned the channel to his security camera. When he saw that it was Renee standing outside, he flicked the channel back to Empire. Brave got up and walked over to the door. He unlocked it and opened it.

"Wassup, girl. A nigga done dozed off. I forgot I even told you to come by," he said, wiping the sleep out of his eyes.

Renee stood there unaware of what her next move should be. Here it was again that Brave was into her but, then, the next minute, he was curving her.

"Do you want me to leave? I can call the cab back," she said.

Brave screwed up his face. "You took a cab all the way here? That shit had to be a few dollars."

Renee nodded yes. "Yeah, it was, but it's cool," she assured, knowing damn well she didn't have the extra money to splurge.

She had put herself on a certain budget and, if it wasn't mandatory, then she wasn't supposed to put money out for it. Renee wanted to put a down payment on a house someday, and if she kept saving the money she made at the boutique, then her dream was going to come true very soon one day.

"Damn ma, well come in. I don't mean to have you just standing out here." He stepped back to let her in.

Renee walked in and was amazed by how nice his house was. Brave gave her the bachelor type of vibe, but his home was clearly warm and cozy, as if he had a family stashed away somewhere.

"Your house is beautiful," she told him.

Brave closed the door and walked back over to the couch. "Thanks. It's nothin' though," he said as he sat down.

"Nothing? Stop it. Whoever decorated ya house did a damn good job," she complimented.

Brave screwed up his face at her, just like he did before. "So, because I'ma hood nigga, I don't have the means to do this shit myself?"

"Oh, I didn't mean it that way. I just thought, ugh, just forget it," she gave up.

Brave started to laugh. Renee was a nervous wreck when she was around him and it was funny as hell to him.

"You can sit down, ya know," he said.

Renee put her purse on the table and took a seat next to Brave. *He smells so good*, she thought.

"You hungry? I got some food in there that I ordered before you got here," he said.

"I can tell by the sauce on your lip and the plate on the table," Renee laughed.

Brave laughed as well and then got up to go in the kitchen. Renee took it upon herself to follow him, so she could get a mini tour of the rest of the house.

"You sure you not hungry?" Brave asked as he got a paper towel and wet it.

"Nah, I'm good."

Brave wiped his mouth and looked towards Renee, who had taken a seat at the table.

"You good? I hope you not one of those fake ass bitches who act like they can't eat in front of a guy. If that's you, then shorty, I'm tellin' you now, you might as well call that cab back because I ain't for the fake shit."

Brave gave it to her straight raw with no chaser. He would rather have a female show him who she was up front, then to put on a front. If you were a hoe, then be a hoe, and if you were a gold digger, then be a gold digger. But, one thing he wasn't for was a nigga or female acting like something they're not.

"No, it's not like that. I just wasn't really hungry since I ate a little before I got here, but I don't mind take something to drink though." Renee tried her best to smooth things over.

Brave threw the paper towel in the trash and then went to the fridge. He opened it and left the door wide open.

"Get whatever you want," he said and went back into the living room.

Renee got up and went to the sink to wash her hands. She dried them and then went to the fridge and looked at the varieties of juices and sodas that Brave had. She settled for a Pepsi and closed the refrigerator door.

"Ya fridge packed like the first of the month," she joked while taking a seat next to him.

"Yeah, but I barely cook. I keep that shit filled, just in case I have a few homies over for like a lil bbq or somethin', feel me?"

Renee nodded yes. "Yeah, I feel you," she said as she took a sip of her soda.

"You got a lot of leaning to do ma."

Renee slowly pulled the can from her lips. She wondered was he referring to her drinking out of a can, instead of cup.

"I forgot to get a glass, sorry," she said.

"Fuck that, that shit ain't bout nothin'. I'm talkin' about you not being confident and learning how to not say the wrong shit at the wrong time," he said.

Renee put on a confused look. "Huh? What do you mean?"

Brave put his hand behind his head and got comfortable. "You felt some way about how shit went last night?"

Renee was embarrassed and she grew uncomfortable. She thought she could trust Harmony, but it seemed like her friendship with Brave was way more important than the bond they were trying to build.

"Hmm, what else did Harmony tell you?" she said was frustration in her voice.

Brave licked his lips. "See, that shit right there. That's the shit I'm talkin' bout. We gon' clear some shit up right now. First and foremost, don't assume shit when it comes to me. Harmony ain't tell me shit and, if she did, then it wouldn't mean nothin' because I already would have peeped it."

"I'm just saying she's the only one I talked to last night."

Brave put his hand up in an 'I don't care' manner. He knew how women were and not only that; he watched her break down in the club's parking lot.

"I don't give a fuck if you talked to Jesus last night. Shit, if a nigga gon' find out somethin', then that's just what it is," he said.

Renee sat her soda down on the table. She was getting aggravated because of how hard Brave was being on her. He didn't know her from a hole in the wall and here he was coming at her like he had the right to.

"Maybe I should go," she said as she got up.

"Nah, maybe you should sit that ass down. You good at runnin' away from shit, I see and, if you tryna get close to a nigga, then that shit right there ain't gon' fly ma."

After hesitating for a moment, Renee finally sat back down. She didn't know whether to like Brave or to run far, far away from him. He definitely wasn't like any of the men she'd dealt with before, and it kind of turned her on in a way.

"What do you want from me?" she asked.

He shrugged his shoulders. "I don't want shit from you, personally, but I am tryna see what you about."

"Oh, so you wanna fuck? Typical." She shook her head.

"To be honest, I could have you ass up and face down right now or suckin' my dick if I wanted to because a nigga horny as shit right now. But, I just wanted to have some good conversation wit' you because that's somethin' I don't get from females these days. That's what I mean when I say you say the wrong shit at the wrong time but, then again, if you want me to fuck you and send you on ya way, then let me know."

Renee couldn't even respond right away. Brave was so real and raw. His whole demeanor was sexy as fuck to her, and what turned her on the most was that he didn't want to fuck her, just like that.

"How old are you?" she changed the subject.

"Thirty-two, why you ask?"

Brave didn't look a day over twenty-five. He definitely took care of himself. He didn't have any bags under his eyes, and his skin was so clear and smooth.

"You look good for your age," she said.

"What?" he laughed. "I'm supposed to look old or somethin'?"

"No, silly. I'm just saying you really take care of yourself. All that soda in ya fridge and ya skin smooth like that?"

"I drink Pepsi ma but not often. I'm more of a juice and water kind of guy, hence my skin." He flexed for her a little. "I also don't stress. I did too much of that shit back in my teen days."

Renee was impressed just by the little bit that she heard. She opened her mouth to ask another question, but Brave cut her off.

"How many kids you got?"

Oh boy. I knew this was coming, she thought.

"I got three kids. My oldest is ten, my middle child is seven, and my youngest is six," she told him.

"Sheessh! You got yaself a lil football team."

Renee playfully mushed him on his arm. "Shut up! No, I don't. I know it sounds bad, but they're really good kids. But, I guess you wouldn't know that, considering you don't fuck with women with kids. That must mean you're not good with kids, since you don't have none or want anything to do with them."

"You right. I don't," Brave answered nonchalantly.

He wanted to hurt Renee's feelings at that moment because once again, she said the wrong thing at the wrong time. For the rest of the day, Brave made it his mission to get as much out of Renee as possible. Some questions she was hesitant to answer, but he had to admit; he really did enjoy the conversation they had. Renee was a cool chick with a battered past. Brave figured he could keep her around for some time and see how things played out. He also had plans on fucking her the next time he saw her and, by the way she acted the first time they chilled, Brave knew he was going to be able to smash.

Chapter Sixteen

Jasmin had called Kaotic over ten times that Monday morning. She had taken an early lunch just to spend some time with him, considering she hadn't seen or heard from him since the small argument they got into, and that was two weeks ago. For as many times as she called, not once did he respond. Tears rolled down her face as she stood in front of the boutique. She had made one hell of a decision to prove her love to him and, now that he wasn't responding to her, she wondered whether or not it was the right thing to do.

Looking down at her phone, she decided to give it one more attempt. Instead of calling Kaotic, she texted him and prayed that he responded.

Jasmin: *Hey baby. I've been calling you all day. I miss you so much. I also have a*

*surprise for you. **Come by the house tonight around 9pm. I love you.***

After pressing the send button, her heart was beating nervously. She wanted Kaotic to know that she loved him more than anything.

"Hey Jasmin, are you okay?" Harmony asked as she walked up.

Jasmin was so lost in her thoughts that she hadn't even realized Harmony was standing there. She quickly wiped her face and fixed herself up.

"Yes, I'm fine. How are you? I didn't think you would be coming in today," Jasmin said, but her response was a bit snobby.

Before Harmony could even think about bucking back at her response, she saw Brave's 2015 silver BMW pull up and her eyes almost popped out of her head when she saw Renee in the passenger side seat.

"What the hell is going on?" Harmony mumbled, as she scratched the back of her head in confusion.

She had never known of Brave taking a liking to any woman that fast, let alone have them riding shotgun in his car. She eagerly watched him pull in front of the boutique. Harmony couldn't wait until

Renee got out of the car, so she could get the tea on what was going on between the two.

"Thank you so much. For the ride and for a wonderful night." Renee smiled.

"This shit ain't about nothin'. Make sure you give that money to ya babysitter. You gon' need her more often," he said with a wink.

Renee melted as she nodded her head and got out of the car. She was blushing something serious and was smiling from ear to ear when she walked up to where Harmony and Jasmin was standing.

"Well, good morning. Someone is beaming today!" Harmony greeted her.

Renee playfully waved her off. "Good morning Harmony. How are you?"

"Oh, I'm doing just fine. The question is, how are you Ms. Thang?"

Renee was glowing and there was nothing she could do to hide it. It was as if Brave put a spell on her because all she could think about was him and he had just left. Renee didn't respond to Harmony, but something told her to look towards Jasmin. If looks could kill, then Renee would be dead, and Harmony peeped it as well. It kind of made her feel like Renee was telling the truth that night.

"Hey Jasmin. Why don't you take the rest of the day off? It looks like you need to relax a little," Harmony threw shade in the politest way possible.

"Thanks because I damn sure need it." Jasmin walked away from the ladies and got in her car without looking back. She sped off violently, and Renee couldn't help but flip her the bird, hoping she saw her.

"Girl, stop it."

"Ugh, I can't stand her, Harmony." Renee rolled her eyes.

"Don't worry about that. Let's go inside and talk because I need to know all the details!"

Harmony and Renee went into the store and headed straight for her office. Crystal shot a nasty look at Renee as she walked by. She was disgusted by how close the two were becoming. When they got inside Harmony's office, she closed the door.

"Harmony, first, I want to say thank you. Brave is thorough as fuck and I love it!"

"Shhh." Harmony put her finger to her mouth. "No one else needs to hear you. But, anyway, you're welcome Renee. I've never seen you like this before. It makes me happy to see you happy."

"I am happy and I know we're just friends, but it feels good to have a male friend that isn't trying to take advantage of me. We pretty much talked about everything yesterday and, noooo, we didn't have sex. We just had some really good conversation, and we ended up falling asleep," she explained.

Clap. Clap. Clap.

Harmony gave her a dramatic round of applause. "I told you all you had to do was relax and be confident baby girl. I'm really happy for you because Brave is a good guy."

"I know, but it's going to be difficult taking things further because he definitely doesn't seem like the relationship type."

Ring. Ring. Ring.

The ringing of the phone interrupted their conversation.

"Hello, Love and Harmony Boutique. Harmony speaking," she greeted the person on the other end.

"Hello Harmony, this is Rachel. How are you? I'm just calling to let you know that the meeting with

Mr. Ford will be the 25th of this month. Is that day okay?" Rachel asked.

Harmony was smiling so big at the news she just received. "Yes! The 25th is fine," she confirmed.

"Great! I'll be sending you a confirmation email. It will have the date, time, address, and your plane ticket all in one."

Harmony placed her hand over her mouth. She couldn't believe this was really happening for her and that she was about to meet the American fashion designer, screen writer, and film producer. This was definitely a dream come true for her.

"Oh, this is wonderful! Thank you so much Rachel!"

"You are very welcome Harmony. Have a great day."

"You too, Rachel." Harmony ended the call.

Click.

"What was all of that about?" Renee asked.

Harmony sat down at her desk and placed a strand of hair behind her ear. "When I said there were going to be some changes, I meant it. That phone call confirmed it all. I'll be having a meeting with Tom Ford the end of this month. We are collabing on a design. I'm telling you, Renee, you continue to work hard and you will have everything you desire. That's a promise because I'm a witness to it all."

"Congratulations Harmony! You deserve it. I swear, you're my inspiration," Renee spoke honestly.

Harmony was flattered. She was glad to be that role model for Renee. They talked for another hour before Renee actually got to work. Harmony was so stuck on cloud nine that she totally forgot to check the footage from her security cameras like she intended to. Little did she know, that little mistake was going to cost her a lot sooner or later.

Chapter Seventeen

When Jasmin got home earlier, she didn't waste any time deep cleaning her house and cooking dinner. She wanted everything to be special when Kaotic came by, but here it was 10:00 p.m. and she was calling Kaotic's phone again. She shook her head when he didn't answer. She sat at her kitchen table surrounded by a variety of food. She had expensive champagne and a sexy piece of lingerie on.

Knock. Knock. Knock.

Jasmin damn near jumped out of the chair, trying to get to the door. She quickly unlocked it and slung it up.

"Baby!" She jumped into his arms like a high school girl.

Kaotic gave her a fake smile. He wasn't in the mood for her or her son tonight, but the way Jasmin was beating down his line, he decided to stop by and see what she wanted.

"Wassup? Why you calling my phone like you ain't got no sense?" he asked, pushing her to the side and walking into the house.

Jasmin closed the door and followed behind him. "Because I wanted to spend some time with you. It's been two weeks since we last saw each other."

Kaotic took a seat at the kitchen table. "What's your point? I told you before, I ain't got time for ya bullshit or that dumb ass lil boy you call a son."

Jasmin bit her tongue. She ignored what Kaotic said and began to fix him a plate of the meal she cooked: curry oxtails, baked macaroni and cheese, along with some cabbage. Kaotic's mouth watered when she sat his plate down in front of him.

"I have something I want to tell you," she said as she poured him a glass of Moet.

Kaotic picked up his fork and dove into his food. Every bite was a taste of heaven to him. That was one thing he really liked about Jasmin; she could cook her ass off.

"Kay, you don't have to worry about Sam anymore. I sent him to live with a relative. I know he can be a pain in an ass at times, which is why I sent him away. We can spend time a lot more now and you don't have to worry about seeing his face," Jasmin said.

She was referring to her sixteen-year-old autistic son. Kaotic looked at her in shock because he couldn't believe she went that far, just to keep him around. Nonetheless, the bitch was stupid and that turned him on. It let Kaotic know that she was willing to do any and everything to keep him around and she was the type of woman he needed on his team, just in case he needed someone to do his dirty work.

"Shit bae, that was deep. You don't know how much that mean to a nigga like me." He leaned over and kissed her, something he barely did because he didn't want to seem like the mushy type. Jasmin placed her hand on the side of his face and kissed him passionately.

"Let's go to the bed room," she purred.

She got up from the table and led Kaotic to the back room. There was a candle burning on the nightstand, which gave the dark room a cozy glow. Jasmin removed Kaotic's shirt and then unbuckled his jeans. She was trying to be romantic, but she was killing his vibe.

"Fuck all that dumb shit. Pull that dick out and suck it," he demanded.

Jasmin got on her knees and did as she was told. She released his dick from his boxers and put it in her mouth. After playing with it a little, he was fully erect. She teased the head as she took both hands and gently massaged his dick.

"Sssss," he moaned.

Slurrrp!

She swallowed him whole, causing a slurping sound, and then spit him back out. Jasmin bobbed her head back and forth on his manhood. She was trying her best to take things slow and be passionate with him, but Kaotic didn't have time for that. He grabbed the back of her head roughly and made her gag on his dick.

"Yeah, choke on that shit."

Jasmin pushed at his thighs, trying to get him to release his grip, but he did no such thing. Slob and pre-cum dripped down the sides of her mouth and her eyes teared up. Kaotic's dick got harder, the more he dominated Jasmin.

Plop!

He pulled his dick out of her mouth. "Get up," he ordered.

Jasmin got up and attempted to wrap her arms around Kaotic, but he pushed her away and bent her over the bed. He ripped the lingerie off her ass and spread her ass cheeks.

"Ooooh!" she gasped as he slid his dick deep inside her pussy.

Kaotic took hold of her head and fucked her hard.

Slap. Slap. Slap. Slap.

There was no passion or remorse for the dick down he was giving Jasmin. He rammed his dick inside her fast and hard, just so he could get a quick nut because when it came to sex, that's all she was worth to him.

"Oh, you hurting this pussy baby! Yes! Right there!" Jasmin gasped.

Whap! Whap! Whap!

Kaotic smacked her ass a few times and then pushed deep inside her. "Urgh!"

Kaotic collapsed on top of Jasmin's back as he released his warm semen in her pussy. His body jerked while he tried to get in a few more strokes. Jasmin laid flat on her stomach, taking all of him in. She didn't care how rough he fucked her; as long as she was the woman he was dicking down, that's all that mattered.

"You liked that, didn't you?" she asked.

Kaotic rolled over and got under the blanket. He was still breathing hard. Jasmin joined him under the comforter and snuggled up under him.

"Come on now. Chill with all that," he said.

"Kay, don't act like that. We had a good dinner and we just fucked. The least you can do is cuddle with me. I did go all out for you tonight," she reminded him.

Kaotic brushed her off and turned on his right side. He was full and tired and he had business to take care of tomorrow, so boo loving was not an option. Silence filled the room and, soon after, Jasmin heard a light snore. Her attempt to cuddle with Kaotic worked because she wrapped her arm around him while he laid on his side. She gave his back little pecks all over as she listened to him sleep.

Jasmin fell more in love with Kaotic each day and she could see them having a good future together, if he just let her be there for him like she wanted to.

"Baby," she called him.

When he didn't answer her, she gently tapped him on the shoulder.

"Kay, wake up."

"Huh? What you want girl?" he asked.

"I've been thinking. Maybe if you tried looking for your mother, you might not be so angry. You might be at peace and be able to deal with Sam a little better," she suggested.

Kaotic had been in and out of the system. He knew little to nothing about his mother, but he knew she was still alive. He never thought about reaching out to her and, to be honest, he didn't give a fuck. He felt like Jasmin was crossing the line by getting into his business, regardless if he told her about him or not. It wasn't her place, nor was it the time.

"Bitch, mind ya business. Don't worry about what the fuck I need to be doing!" he snapped.

Jasmin sat up on the bed. She knew that she had hit a nerve because he popped off on her instantly.

"Kay, I'm not trying to be all up in your business. I'm just worried about you. I really am. I love you so much and I just want what's best for you. I think you're holding in a lot of anger, due to you not knowing. Please, just find out why your mother gave you up. It don't take but a few clicks on the internet to find someone and reach out to them," she explained.

Kaotic ignored Jasmin. He didn't respond and he was hoping that she left the situation alone because if she kept on, he was definitely leaving before he knocked her the fuck out. Jasmin must have been reading his mind because she laid back down and wrapped her arm back around him. Kaotic found himself up most of the night thinking about what she said, but he damn sure wasn't going to let her know that she was right. He never gave any woman that kind of lead way. However, he did make a mental note to do some research about where he came from, and he was going to do that as soon as possible.

Chapter Eighteen

Three days later, it was Thursday afternoon and Harmony was closing the shop early. She had stayed open for almost twenty-four hours and made a killing because of the Kevin Gates' bash tonight. The ladies were in and out of her boutique since last night and, although she enjoyed satisfying her customers and getting those coins, she couldn't front and act like she didn't need a break. So, her plans were to close the shop early and head home to spend time with her husband, until he had to leave. As she was gathering up a few folders and her purse from the office, she heard a ding, which let her know that someone had walked in her store.

She quickly rushed out of her office to see who walked in, considering it was clear that the store was closing. When she walked out, she saw Kaotic.

"Um, what the hell are you doing here?" she asked.

"I was in the area and decided to stop by," he told her.

Harmony folded her arms across her chest. She rolled her neck as she talked because she wasn't feeling how their first encounter went down.

"Look, I don't know what the fuck your problem is, but you don't be rolling up in here like you own shit. If you wanted to stop by, then you should've text or called. I'm sure you got my number," she shot back.

She was pissed that she had given him her number and he never bothered to reach out to her. It was as if he just did it to prove that he could get it.

"Ooouuu. Somebody seems a little upset," he laughed. He walked closer to where Harmony was standing and that was just a few inches away from her office door.

"Nigga, you is not cute. But, anyway, as you can see, I'm closed so come at another time."

Kaotic was now face to face with Harmony. "Why you playin' like you don't want me?" he asked.

Before Harmony could respond, Kaotic had his arms wrapped around her waist and he was grabbing her ass. His touch was rough but gentle at the same time.

"What are you-"

He stopped her in mid-sentence by kissing her. His scent made her pussy went and, at that moment, Harmony was in total bliss. It was as if she couldn't stop anything that was taking place, and she was having an outer body experience. It was just Kaotic's luck that Harmony wore a dress that day because he reached underneath her dress and ripped off her thong, throwing it on the floor.

Kaotic unbuckled his jeans and picked Harmony up. His dick was already hard and her pussy was dripping wet. His slid her onto his throbbing dick and bounced her up and down.

"Oh my God!" Harmony gasped as he touched her soul with his dick. She wrapped her arms around his neck and held on for dear life because Kaotic was taking her on a ride. He walked into her office without pulling his dick out or putting her down. Kaotic laid her on the small sofa that was in her office and pushed her legs back.

"You sexy as hell ma," he said, leaning forward to share his tongue with her.

When he was done kissing her, he went back to laying the pipe. He looked down and watched his dick go in and out of her and bit his lip, while her creamy cum coated his dick.

"Ka-Kaotic, I can't do this!" she moaned while she tried to push him back. The dick felt too good, but she finally realized what she was doing. She pushed Kaotic back with force this time and closed her legs.

"What the fuck you doing?" he asked.

"I can't fucking do this! I have a husband. I can't do no shit like this. I can't even believe it got this far." She was pissed at herself.

Harmony went to her purse that was sitting on the desk and got out a few baby wipes. She cleaned herself off and fixed her hair. "You need to leave and never come back. I can't ruin my marriage for some temporary dick," she said.

Kaotic stood up and put his dick back in his pants. Harmony was definitely tripping in his eyes, but it didn't matter because he already had a taste of her and she had a taste of him. He knew they were bound to see one another again.

"So, you really want me to leave?" he asked.

Harmony ran her fingers through her hair in a stressed manner. She was beyond frustrated with her own actions. Never in a million years would she have thought that she would cheat on her husband. The man she vowed to spend the rest of her life with. She knew she had to keep this little incident a secret because if Chaos ever found out that she cheated on him, he was going to kill her.

"Kaotic, please leave. Just please," she begged.

Kaotic smirked at her and nodded. "Cool, but this won't be the last time I see you, beautiful. You can believe that," he said before walking out of her office.

Harmony turned to gather her things. She had to hurry up and close before Kaotic thought to make another attempt. She was so busy trying to close the store and get home to Chaos that she never realized Kaotic took her ripped thongs as a souvenir.

Chapter Nineteen

Later on that night, Chaos was sitting on the couch relaxing before he had to get going. Harmony was sitting right next to him, sipping out of her wine glass that was filled with Henny.

"Babe, how much do you love me?" she asked.

After the bullshit she pulled earlier, Harmony had to do something to keep her mind off the mistake she made. She had been walking on egg shells all day, and she tried her best not to act different. When she got home from work, she was so thankful that Chaos was busy. That gave her time to take a hot bath and get herself right, just in case he decided he wanted to fuck.

Harmony looked over at Chaos, who was too busy in his phone to respond to the question she just asked, and that pissed her off. She was praying that he wasn't ignoring her because he may have found out that she cheated on him. But, Chaos ignoring her should have been the least of her worries because if he knew what she did, ignoring her wouldn't even be in his vocabulary.

Whap!

She smacked him on his arm to get his attention.

"Damn bae, I heard you and, furthermore, why the fuck would you ask a question like that? I tell you I love you damn near every day," he said.

"No, you don't. You always say love you more or love you too. It's never I love you and, quite frankly, I'm tired of that shit," Harmony confessed.

Although she was tired of it, the Henny was definitely talking for her. Harmony didn't want to bring up such topic with her knowing that Chaos had to work that night. She liked for him to be stress free so that he could be on his P's and Q's. Harmony wanted Chaos to be alert at all times, especially when it came to big events like the one he and Brave was doing that night.

"Harmony, chill. Don't start that shit right now. I swear, you actin' mad weird right now, like you did some shit. Harmony, if I find out you doin' some grimy shit, on God, I'ma put two in ya head. You know I love you, so all this shit you doin' is suspect as hell," he told her.

Pssh!

Harmony sucked her teeth and rolled her eyes. She felt like Chaos was full of bullshit, trying to flip the script on her.

"Get the fuck outta here. Don't flip this shit and act like I'm doing something when I'm not!" she was lying through her teeth. "You can't even look me in my fuckin' face and say, Harmony, I love you. That shit don't count." She waved him off and took another sip of her Henny.

Chaos was texting away, all while Harmony was giving him the third degree. Whenever Harmony felt like Chaos was ignoring her, her feelings got extremely hurt.

"Chaos, are you serious right now?" She gazed at him through low eyes. She waited for a response but got none. Harmony got up and pretended to go in the kitchen, but she was really peeking in Chaos' phone. Her body got hot all over, and her nostrils were flared when she saw the name Brittany across the screen.

A random ass bitch, she thought.

Harmony shook her head in disgust as she walked back around the couch and sat down. She grabbed the Hennessy off the glass coffee table and attempted to pour herself another generous glass.

Sloosh!

"Hahaha muthafucka!" Harmony laughed and took off upstairs.

Twenty

"What the fuck!" Chaos stormed up the stairs, hopping up two steps at a time into the master bedroom, and looked at Harmony as she laughed hysterically.

Harmony had just thrown a fifth of Henny on him and he was beyond pissed. She took it as a joke because she knew just how to get under his skin and bring him out of character.

"Don't what the fuck me. Who was that bitch texting your phone?" she asked through pursed lips, with her arms folded across her chest.

"Wasn't no bitch texting my phone. The fuck you coming at my neck for anyway? You got niggas coming at you on a daily!"

Harmony waved him off. It was just like Chaos to flip the script on her but, over the years of dealing

with him, Harmony had gotten used to it, so it wasn't as easy for him to get to her as it was before.

"I don't wanna hear that shit. You either gon' tell me who the fuck that bitch is, or I will GPS her number and I'll find out who the fuck she is myself," Harmony warned.

Chaos wiped his hand down his face as he looked at his woman. He knew she was good to pull up on a bitch if need be. He didn't want anyone to get their ass beat over an innocent text message, so he just confessed.

"Baby, it wasn't like that. She's just an old friend who decided to hit me up and see how I was doing. You need to stop fucking tripping. You know you my one and fucking only. Ya guts is the only one's I'm beating down, believe that," Chaos said as he pulled his wife beater over his head and threw it on the floor.

She watched as he unbuckled his jeans and dropped them to his knees, along with his brief boxers. His thick nine-and-a-half-inch anaconda stood at attention. She just knew he was about to punish her pussy by the way it was staring at her.

"The fuck you over there drooling for? You ain't getting none of this good dick after what you done did. I'm about to hop in the tank. As a matter of fact, sit down on the bed and think about what you've done." Chaos headed towards the bathroom doorway before he heard Harmony suck her teeth.

He laughed and went into the bathroom, shutting the door behind him. He knew she was pissed because she couldn't get any dick, but she was just going to have to be mad because he had things to do at the club later. Chaos let the water run over his body for a few before lathering up his wash cloth with some of his AXE body wash. He cleaned himself from head to toe and then rinsed his body. He turned the water off and stepped out of the shower, wrapping a towel around his waist. Chaos wiped the fog off the mirror and admired himself. His fresh line-up he had gotten earlier had him looking like new money. But, that was nothing new because even on his worse day, he looked like a million bucks. Chaos grabbed his toothbrush and toothpaste and quickly brushed his teeth. When he was done, he swished some mouth wash around in his mouth and then spit it out.

"Ahhhh," he made a noise as he stuck out his tongue.

Chaos walked back into the bedroom to find Harmony watching tv.

"Where you going?"

"To the club. Don't ask me a question you already know the answer to."

Harmony rolled her eyes. She watched Chaos drop his towel and expose that pretty chocolate dick of his. The veins were bulging as it stood out at attention. He rubbed Cocoa Butter on his body and then threw on a clean pair of boxer briefs.

"You need to control your dick. That's why those bitches always on you because your dick always hard."

Chaos chuckled. "Kind of explains the way I got you."

Harmony threw the remote control to the side and hopped off the bed. A few steps later, she was standing in back of Chaos, blowing nothing but hot air as she fussed at him.

"Don't say no stupid shit like that nigga! I def' wasn't on your dick like these thirsty, popcorn ass

bitches be. I'm above all. Don't even compare me to them whack ass bitches!"

Chaos smiled inside because he was pushing her buttons and he knew it. *Bet she won't throw shit else on me*, he thought.

"Ssss, ouch!" he winced in pain when Harmony pinched him in his side. It was like she could hear his thoughts. The pinch was followed by a punch in his back.

"Stop fucking hitting me. Then, when I knock your fucking head, off I'll be wrong." He slipped into a pair of red, knee-length basketball shorts with black lining and a black, v-neck t-shirt.

"I wish you would hit me! I wish you would nigga!" she taunted.

Chaos ignored her and put on his white and black Nike socks, along with his black Adidas slippers.

"Why the fuck you got on Nike socks with Adidas?"

Chaos glanced at her. "Because I'm that nigga and I can do that. Anymore fucking questions?"

He wasn't big on following the rules. He always stepped outside of the box and did what other niggas

was afraid to do. Clearly, he was the type that would wear two different brand clothing and not give the slightest fuck about it.

"I guess so but, anyway, what time you gon' be back?" Harmony looked at her cellphone and saw that it was already going on 8:30 p.m.

She couldn't stand when Chaos went to the club, let alone at night time because that's when all the wanna-be thugs would come there and try to act up. Most of all, that's when the bitches got extremely out of pocket because the majority of the ballers came in at night.

"I'm not sure at the moment. You know tonight is Kevin Gates' party, so I gotta get there now to finish puttin' shit together."

"So, why you got on lounging clothes?" she asked.

"Brave already got my outfit at the club. I wanted to go to the club in something comfortable because I gotta finish puttin' shit together, like I just said."

Harmony sighed because she wanted him to stay in with her tonight, but this was one of the biggest parties he'd had, so she had to let him handle his business.

Chaos put on some of his Versace cologne and then turned around to face his lady. He walked up on her and grabbed the sides of her face with his hands in an aggressive but romantic manner.

"You know I love your wild ass, right?" He shared his tongue with her.

Harmony took it with no problem. She loved the taste of him, but her wants caused her to betray him time and time again. "Yeah, I know, but you better get going. The sooner you leave, the quicker you will return."

Chaos gave her another peck on the lips. "Yeah, I hear you." He walked out of the bedroom and she followed behind him. "Give me a chance to peep things and I'll hit you up in a little while."

Harmony handed him his keys to his 2015 all-white Bentley and kissed him once more. "Alright, make sure you do. I love you."

"Love you more." Chaos left out of the house.

Harmony looked out of their bay window and watched as he got in his car and pulled off. She bit her bottom lips, watching his car until the tail light was out of sight. She planned on telling Chaos the

truth that night, but she couldn't muster up the strength to do it.

I'll just do it when he gets back, she thought.

She plopped down on the couch and cuddled up in fetal position, reaching for the remote on the end table and powering on the tv. She settled to watch VH1's hit movie, The Breaks, before dropping the remote by the couch on the floor. Harmony laid down and drifted off to sleep, not realizing she was tired.

An hour later, she was awakened by the ringing of the house phone.

Ring. Ring. Ring

Harmony hadn't even realized she had fallen asleep. She sat up on the couch and wiped the drool from her cheek. She instantly became aggravated because of the loud ringing. It was rare that their house phone rung but, when it did, the noise bothered her.

"Hello!" she yelled into the phone. Her voice cracked from the left over sleep.

"Yo, Harmony, Chaos got shot! I mean, that nigga got shot bad. He bleeding bad. Man, all this shit is bad!" Brave said in a panicked tone.

Harmony's heart dropped into her stomach. She couldn't believe the news she'd just received. At that moment, the room started to spin, her head got dizzy, and her vision became cloudy. Her mouth watered and she swallowed hard to keep the vomit that was forcing its way up, down.

She knew there was a reason she didn't want him to go to the club that night. Her gut told her that something would happened, but she didn't listen. Harmony didn't know that, when she told Chaos she loved him, it would be her last time able to do it.

Questions For Readers & Book Club

1. What do you think of Harmony's character?

2. Do you think Harmony was too hard up on Renee?

3. What do you think of Chaos character?

4. Do you think Chaos was wrong for spending so much time at the club?

5. Did Harmony take out her frustrations on Renee?

6. Was Renee wrong for having such an attitude all the time?

7. Do you think Renee has something up her sleeve or is she loyal?

8. Does Jasmin know that her boss is sleeping with her man?

9. What do you think about Kaotic?

10. Do you think there is any relation between Chaos and Kaotic?

11. Is Harmony wrong for stepping outside of her marriage and looking for love in other places?

12. What do you think about Brave's character?

13. What do you think Brave's actions will be after Chaos is hurt?

14. Who do you think shot Chaos and why?

Stay tuned for the answers to any unanswered questions from part one. Harmony & Chaos part 2, coming soon. If you are an online book club that is interested in having a book discussion you can find my email at the beginning of the book.

Much Love,

Reds Johnson

**Get the entire
HARMONY & CHAOS COLLECTION
Today!**

Available Now!
www.iamredsjohnson.com

Reds Johnson also known as Anne Marie, is a twenty-three-year-old independent author born and raised in New Jersey. She started writing at the age of nine years old, and ever since then, writing has been her passion. Her inspirations were Danielle Santiago, and Wahida Clark. Once she came across their books; Reds pushed to get discovered around the age of thirteen going on fourteen.

To be such a young woman, the stories she wrote hit so close to home for many. She writes urban, romance, erotica, bbw, and teen stories and each book she penned is based on true events; whether she's been through it or witnessed it. After being homeless and watching her mother struggle for many years, Reds knew that it was time to strive harder. Her passion seeped through her pores so she knew that it was only a matter of time before someone gave her a chance.

Leaping head first into the industry and making more than a few mistakes; Reds now has the ability to take control of her writing career. She is on a new path to success and is aiming for bigger and better opportunities.

Visit my website www.iamredsjohnson.com

MORE TITLES BY REDS JOHNSON

SILVER PLATTER HOE 6 BOOK SERIES

HARMONY & CHAOS 6 BOOK SERIES

MORE TITLES BY REDS JOHNSON

NEVER TRUST A RATCHET BITCH 3 BOOK SERIES

TEEN BOOKS

A PROSTITUTE'S CONFESSIONS SERIES

CLOSED LEGS DON'T GET FED SERIES

MORE TITLES BY REDS JOHNSON

OTHER TITLES BY REDS JOHNSON

Made in the USA
Monee, IL
10 November 2022